FOGLIFTER

CREDITS

Editor-in-Chief, *Foglifter*
Luiza Flynn-Goodlett

Managing Poetry Editor	**Managing Hybrid/CNF Editor**	**Managing Fiction Editor**
Michal MJ Jones	Miah Jeffra	Damitri Martinez

Assistant Poetry Editor	**Guest Editors**	**Assistant Fiction Editors**
Charlie Neer	Nefertiti Asanti	Wesley Cohen
	Jody Chan	N/A Oparah
		Milo Todd

Development Director	**Production Manager**	**Production Editor**
Jessie Galloway	Miah Jeffra	Jason Lipeles

Community Manager	**Web Manager**	**Distribution Manager**
Misha Ponnuraju	Irwan bin Iskak	Chad Koch

Contributing Editors

Melton Cartes	Stacy Nathaniel Jackson	Celeste Chan
Danny Thanh Nguyen	D.A. Powell	Sandhya Ramnan

Book Layout and Design	Miah Jeffra Jason Lipeles
Copy Editor	Susan Calvillo
Cover Artwork	from *Mouthpiece* by Lemia Monét Bodden Courtesy of the artist

ISSN: 2470-3443

ISBN: 978-1-7369045-3-4

Vol. 6 Issue 2
2021

Foglifter is published twice yearly in San Francisco, California.

Foglifter is exclusively a publication of Foglifter Press. All correspondence may be addressed to 1200 Clay Street #4, San Francisco, CA 94108. Details at www.foglifterpress.com.

Table of Contents

Poetry

PROSE

HYBRID

INTERVIEW

CANDACE WILLIAMS

Owed

watching my mother balance   the family checkbook   seemed like the writing of odes:
some on-sale bananas   that dress   your bike laid away   there was always something owed

my senior english teacher assigned neruda   told me he was the world's passion: he sings to socks
praises tomatoes   forces himself into a woman   writes *There was no language*   for this dark ode

school was the bloody gash of sifting   my brown 300 lb frame   through pale mesh   I joined crew
we scrimmaged on American Lake   I waited cold starboard   dropped oar to blue   I rowed

I can remember the two times I've made white men cry   I was 19 on a doorstep   26 in a boardroom
the easiest way toward white sobs   is the precision of a black woman breaking down   what she's owed

I almost killed my father three times in an the space of an hour   at the last near-miss turning   he cried:
Candace pull over now   give me the wheel   you'll be too early for your date with death   down the road

Candace Williams

From "The Dark Diary"

I.

The day was ending in stained light—the west
glowing white without rays, without heat: sudden death
by touch of brooding men. A change came over
the water. We looked vivid in august light

as the phrase goes: *terror knows ships bear
the sword.* This stir of light is a lurid glare. There is nothing
mysterious: Hours of work. A casual spree. A whole continent
the shell of a cracked nut. The glow brings a haze: misty

halo. But Darkness was here. Darkness, the colour
of kin, of order. White is a bundle of cold tempests:
exile, death—death skulking the air. Darkness survived
the awful climate—the trader savagery: utter savagery

fascination, abomination preaching in European clothes—*efficiency
devotion to efficiency, account administration*: A squeeze.
Brute force. An accident. The conquest of the earth. A sacrifice.
We understand the effect of light on everything: a pitiful

kind of light invading your homes, just a heavenly mission
to civilize you: A white dream. Vast country. A company—
fresh departure. I wouldn't have believed myself but black is asserting
self-respect in some way. The white man expects all

kinds of opportunity: grass growing tall enough to hide
the bones—they were all there. Black men children the cause
of progress: whited sepulchre. We were going to run through
vast white, its light a heavy pale. I found myself

again: I am black and young walking back and forth
guarding the door of Darkness, knitting black
wool for the young and the dead. I said yes
produced a thing. I have a little theory:

my country shall reap from my possession
my observation was not typical. I was also one
of the workers. Light is such rot. I ventured queer—
feeling came to me. I was an imposter: almost black

fringed with white, ran straight like a ruled line
sun whitish with the white idleness of a passenger
my isolation seemed to keep me from the truth of things
mournful, senseless delusion. A momentary contact with reality

you could see from afar—white bodies, faces grotesque
masks. Intense energy an excuse for being there
I saw the mouth speaking English with great precision
and considerable bitterness; I wonder: What becomes god?

A reach? A waste? An evacuation? Continuous noise.
Sunlight drowned all this. I came back black on the face
of a rock, black in file balancing time black force
at work seeing white on the path—white men

being so much (and not particularly tender)
I've had to strike and to fend off. I've had to resist and attack
that's one way of resisting—counting the exact cost
of life blundered into. How insidious the devil—a vast

artificial hole, the purpose of which is philanthropic
desire. I discovered my purpose: black against
light attitudes of pain and despair. Black shadow
fed on unfamiliar food, free as air. The black

flicker in the depths of the orbs: Sister Phantom
in every pose. I didn't want any more loitering
I made haste; set off toward dark eternity. I began
to write again. The noise stopped at the door

the agent was bent over books, making transactions—
the sound of a bell in a Christian country
white men retire at the end of speeches
that originate nothing as though it had been a door

opening into Darkness surrounding truth waiting
patiently for the passing invasion. Various
things happen: cotton bursts into blaze. I approach
the glowdark. I found myself hissing ruin of government

the only real feeling was desire. *A singleness
of purpose*. Who says that? Lots of them. Some even
write. I interrupt the new gang—gang of virtue
the same people who sent light to produce

opportunity. The hissing ascended moonlight's
brute transgressions: telling the manager. Gesticulating
discussing the mysterious reality of concealed life. The hurt
the deep sigh. The false idea of disposition. This papier-mache

mephistopheles poked in. I did try to stop him
the wreck hauled up on the shore. The smell
primeval mud. White man jabbered about himself. A menace
who strayed here. A confounded god knows his fiend

you know I can't bear a lie—I want to forget Europe
and the rest of the bewitched pilgrims. Do you
see the story? It seems to me I am trying
to tell you a dream: a commingling of absurdity

bewilderment, a tremor of struggling revolt
a notion of being captured by the very essence
of light glittering distrubed—the bad habit
the pilgrims empty every rifle they lay

hands on—charmed brutes. A charmed life in the moonlight
glittering empty; a gutter. They never tell
what it really means. I suppose white purpose
is a clattering sleep. My dark figure obscures

the lighted doorway. I did not know of any reason
why we shouldn't—there came an invasion, an infliction
a visitation in white installments. An absurd disorderly
flight of loot, of innumerable stores. They were lugging

a raid against equitable division, human folly
made the spoils of thieving sordid, reckless, cruel
without courage. They seem aware these things are wanted:
tearing treasure out of bowels of their desire.

No moral purpose. Burglars break into safe
enterprise in poor neighborhoods. I had given up
worrying myself about their morals of work.

This poem is an excerpt of an erasure of Joseph Conrad's *Heart of Darkness and the Congo Diary*.

BESSIE F. ZALDÍVAR

Zuihitsu from the violence in my mother's body

1.

My mother is a cartoon. She does not own the rights to her image. ~~Nickelodeon~~ and ~~Disney Junior~~ held a 41-year long legal fight over it. By the time it was resolved she was too old to appeal to young audiences and neither wanted her. They claimed that no one wanted their children to see the stretch marks of three births or hear knees that pop and crack with every inhale. And don't even get me started with the scars business.

The first tell of my mother's cartoonness are her eyelashes: long and thick, from the wet tongues of her eyes to the southern border of her eyebrows. She wouldn't want me to tell you this, but, yes, they're extensions. The second, perhaps most obvious evidence of her cartoonness is her inability to die. Unaired scene: One evening of January 2017, my cartoon mother is dropping off fresh bedsheets at her grandmother's house. She sits in her car. Big, cartoon, black-outlined clouds of smoke exhale through back pipe of her midnight-blue Mitsubishi Outlander. She calls her grandmother to come outside. Because she is a woman in Tegucigalpa, she notices the grey car that parks behind her—the same one that followed her down this dead-end road. She notices the oversized cartoon sign that reads DEAD END with a big red "X" at the beginning of the street. She doesn't turn off her engine, but she does turn off the lights. As if cued by darkness, four men spring from each door of the grey car. Four men dressed exactly the same: black pants, black shirts, black guns, black hats. The men surround her. One man knocks on her window with the mouth of his gun. Thought bubbles pop over my mother's head. They say, *just give them your phone and wallet, Maria, it's what they want.* But a smaller, yet smarter thought bubble disagrees. After all, she has done this many times before. There's a whole season about guns held to her head by men like these.

The man at her door knocks against the window again. The barrel of his gun on the glass promises the end of a sentence without punctuation. He is an impatient man, or rather, he is a man in an impatient line of business. Notice the cartoon lines and exclamation points coming out of his head like a New Year's Eve party hat. They signal his frustration; this is taking too long. He raises the gun to the level of her brain. He pulls the trigger back to his body—a finger motion not so different from reaching to your love's face to flick food crumbs away. And then he shoots.

My mother jumps forward. Hugs the wheel like she hugged me in a hospital bed years ago, when my body was nothing more than an overgrown bullet wet with blood and her insides. One of the men behind the car follows—bang, bang. Remember, she did not turn the car off. She drives away. Bang. Bang. The window breaks. Bang. She drives herself to the hospital. The first bullet had passed through her arm. It is now, in the exact moment I write this and you read it, still in the car. Lodged inside the passenger's door, near the remote control that raises and lowers the window. No one can get it out. Our fingers aren't long or thin enough. It lives in this small hole, in a wall of plastic. It goes with her to work every morning and brings her home at night. It rides my siblings to school. It sleeps in the garage, next to the same house we do.

Here's the thing—I think her eyelashes could reach it. If we looped a rod out of them, if we could really try. With one eyelash we could fish it from inside. Remember: my mother is a cartoon. She won't ever die and her eyelashes are long enough for three more lives. But she doesn't own the rights to her image yet. We don't know who drew her. Only that the American networks don't want her anymore.

•

Naturally, we spend the next few days playing the game of what could have happened. You have played it too. We all have. Either to imagine the worst or dream of the best. What would have happened if she had just opened the door? We think, abduction, taken to the outskirts of Tegucigalpa, rape, murder, body in ditch or river or black trashcan bag. These are the stories we read and see every day. What do you think they wanted? A getaway car. To get away from that? Who do you think they were? Police, she says. Maybe, I don't know. They looked like policemen. How so? I don't know. Their movements. Their clothes. Their bodies. I don't know. The next morning, I count how many people tell my mother she is a miracle, without knowing her, just from a glimpse of the perfectly shaped bullet-width hole at the height of her head. As if they can microscope through it the intentions of her creation. Some add, *God must have big plans for you!* My mother is a cartoon my mother is the end of a sentence with no punctuation my mom is a thought bubble my mother is eyelash extension glue my mother isn't a miracle because miracles own the rights to their image. My mother's eyelashes are tally marks and maybe you can guess what they're counting.

newspaper front pages of tegucigalpa the day after my mother is shot

2.

In Honduras, there are three ways to get rich: drug trafficking, money laundering for drug traffickers, or marrying someone who is a narco and/or cleans the narco's money. This is what they mean when they say we live in a narcoestado. The downside to all paths is, of course, the more-than-occasional murder. But, duh, you can be murdered any day for any reason that has nothing to do with these. Dying your hair the wrong color. Wearing the wrong soccer jersey on the wrong side of the city. Not handing over your phone fast enough. Unmarked and unspoken rules of death fall from our broken-tube showerheads run through our naked bodies, wash down the drain with our dead hair and toenails, travel the length of our cities and pueblos, all the way to the rivers. When it rains, it rains rules of death.

My mother is at the club. I say "the," not "a." There are four in the city. Let's just assume she's at the newest one. She hasn't been shot yet; that won't happen for a few years. My mother is with her friends. A man with a sombrero—like the ones in the framed pictures on the walls of your American Mexican restaurants—approaches her. Puts his hands on her shoulders. Says, *¿quiere bailar?* She's taller than he is. She's way younger. The thought of having her body anywhere near his disgusts her. But she saw him get out of his car—a car of a make she can't pronounce. She saw the bodyguards. She knows a man like that can only have one sort of employment. A man like that is not in the business of hearing no. Especially not from women he wants to stick his penis in. She will have to dance, and, somehow, devise a getaway plan. My mother dances until her back hurts. Her back hurts from all the unspoken rules of death sweating down her dress.

·

My mother's back hurts. She lies on her side. I lie behind her. My bent knees fit into hers like 50-piece puzzle pieces. I am spreading VapoRub on her skin. Here? I say. Lower. Here? To the right. Here? A little up. She coughs. Neither of us has been able to smell or taste anything in days. My sister, my mother's youngest, said she couldn't smell our coffee this morning, either. My mother's fever doesn't break for hours. We are a sweaty bundle of limbs. We are a cloud of tissue paper glued with snort. We are in the middle of a pandemic, and our symptoms are textbook-accurate. It was decided I would come home for three months, when it all started. My mother said, as I booked the ticket, *te necesito aquí, hija. In case something happens.*

Mami, I say, trying to wake her. Mami, we need to drink water. We've been sleeping all day—a thing we never, ever do. Both of us have been up by 6 AM every day of the quarantine. Estas hirbiendo, I say, touching her shoulder. Estas tan caliente. *Maybe my back hurts from the last workout we did,* she says, fever-ridden, fever-dumbed, fever-sleepy. We don't know this yet, because we have no way to know it, but my mother's lungs are Christmas trees wrapped in COVID-focused light bulbs. They brush against her torso walls like pine needles. This is why her back hurts. We have no way of knowing this because as of two weeks ago, the Honduran health system has collapsed. Such an abstract concept wrapped in concrete language. Let me explain the time line.

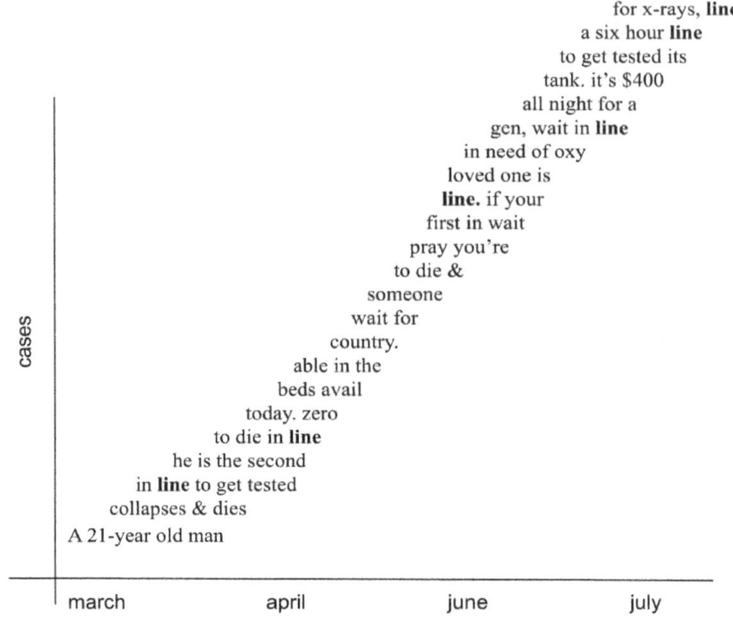

We sniff bottles of everything. Fabuloso. Bleach. Coffee. Even acid. Nothing. Our noses have decided to un-nose scent, to unknown their nose-ness. We eat food like we're chewing cardboard. Everything's tasteless. Our senses are gone. But we're breathing, and that seems like enough.

I don't understand.

What?

How did it get to us? We're so careful.

No one knows how this works. It can get to anyone.

But we never leave the house. We wash our hands.

I know.

We even wash the money!

Ha. Don't say that. It sounds like we're money launderers.

Qué vamos a hacer?

What can we do? Drink water, eat.

What if we need a hospital?

. . . .

What if we need oxygen?

. . . .

What if we need money? I wish we were money launderers

. . . .

Will they let you back into the U.S? If you've had it?
I don't think they care.
What if one of us dies? There's no money for funerals.
…
My back hurts.
Go lay down.

"we even wash the money"

3.

Someone tells my mother that this will all be helpful for her someday if she decides to apply for asylum in another country. Maybe it's after the car shooting, or the domestic violence, or the COVID, or the dengue, or one of the armed robberies without shots. *Todo te va servir,* they tell her. *Para la aplicación.* For the application. What is the application of death in an application for life? What applies as living when you need to apply for it? What is the application of leaving in applying for life?

☐ Check this box if you want to leave/live.

4.

I paint my nails the color of my mother's bulging forehead vein. The one between her eyebrows. The one that rivers from the hem of her hairline and unmouths below her eye. Someone will tell you the vein claimed reign on her face after the coup and someone will say it was right before it, after the first time a man almost killed her. But the only expert on my mother's face is me. Are you picturing the vein Burger King blue or Starbucks green? Perhaps a mixture of both, perhaps Amazon teal. All of these are wrong, of course. The color of my mother's forehead vein is the color of my nails today is the color of my boarding pass from Tegucigalpa to not-Tegucigalpa is the color of my first orgasm is the color of off-brand Tide pods in a Ziploc bag under my bed is the color of my first love's sweat is the color of unread notifications with news about a country that doesn't know of colors not sponsored by American intervention. I live in America today. My mother lives in a country painted in America. My mother is a cartoon. I paint my nails the color of my mother's bulging forehead vein. I am 4,910.6 kilometers away from her. I can't close the space between us without sentencing us to always carrying these veins and nails. We will always carry these veins and these nails.

whatsapp's from my mother, on any given day:

No podés regresar jamás a este país de mierda ✓ ✓

país este   amas   jamas amas   mierda de país a este país ✓ ✓ No✓ ✓
a este país de mierda ✓ ✓ No✓ ✓ imas No podes ✓ ✓ regresar ✓ ✓
regresar✓ ✓ amas este país ✓ ✓ No✓
podes regresar✓ ✓ amas este país de mierda✓ ✓ No✓ ✓
amas este país de mierda ✓ ✓ No podes ✓ ✓   ✓ podes✓
este pais   no   podes✓ amas
jamas podes regresar   este pais   No   a este país de mierda ✓ ✓ No✓ ✓
podes   amas jamas este paisegresar jamas ✓ ✓ a este país de mierda ✓ ✓ No✓ regresar✓
regresar✓ ✓   No amas este pais   podes regresar✓ ✓ amas este país de
No regresar regresa   este pais
podes regresar✓ ✓ amas este país de mierda✓ ✓ No✓ mierda✓ ✓ No✓ ✓ podes✓
jamas   jamas   este pais   es mierda   amas
podes✓   regresar✓ ✓

regresar✓ ✓

5.

My mom es una accidentada, which is not to be confused with being an accident. Her three children were accidents. She was not. She was una accidentada. That's what her mother calls her. Meaning, she is someone who finds herself in accident-type situations constantly. Meaning, she is predisposed to impact. Meaning, she is a cartoon woman and every time the country-shape tractor rolls her over, leaves her flat like stepped-on bubble gum, she unsticks herself from the pavement and her insides re-inflate like the walls of a children's bouncing castle. My mom is una accidentada, since birth, yes. I can make my way down the list of incidents, from the boiling water spill over her chest to the time a literal car ran her over when she was 11. Point is, she is that kind of person that everything seems to happen to.

An accident is an unfortunate, unintentional event resulting in harm. In accidents, intentionality matters. In accidents, the event comes first and the harmed as a result. Una accidentada is a walking harmed that calls unfortunality to her. I don't know if intentions play a part or are beside the point.

For instance, what about that episode, when my cartoon mother says for the first time in a while, to my 17-year-old self and my 8-year-old sister—

But on the way to the movie theater, she stops to buy cheese in a corner store and ends up with a gun pressed to her head, while her two daughters watch from the car. The 8-year-old screams and jumps to the floor—a graveyard of shoe-sole carried crumbs, dirt, mud. This time is not to be confused with the shooting time. On this occasion, no shots were fired. Cartoon mother said, *my daughters are in the car. I will give you my wallet, please.* And that was enough. What is to be said about an accidental-ness that survives? What is to be said of an accidental-ness encoded in your bones, designed to kill you at every turn?

For instance, what about that other episode, the one when my cartoon mother's place of employment is set on fire during a staged protest by the government to distract from American-sponsored electoral fraud, and she is rushed with the rest of the underpaid hotel personnel to the last floor, her future-COVID lungs stuffing with tear gas like a child learning the inside of their mouth is a space that can be filled, and she texts us to let us know she can't text, and we follow the news through WhatsApp forwarded-videos, sitting on our hands, waiting— is her accidentada-ness to be blamed? Or is the first accident birth in an Earth of cartoon people drawn by American hands?

6.

"A word's development is sometimes logical, sometimes not," Merriam-Webster Dictionary tells me when I try to find an answer to how my mother became or was born a cartoon. Cartoon comes from carton, the Spanish and French word for cardboard. Initially, cartoons were not humorous or exaggerated depictions, but fine-art drawings done in hard paper, or cardboard. En carton, on cardboard. If my mother is a cartoon, she is also cardboard. She is also carton. Her nose is the land formed nest of an egg-carton, her arms are the top-flaps of an Amazon delivery box and her torso a Domino's pizza box. Don't you see it? Every body part of my mother's cardboard cartoon body is American-owned.

7.

My mom texts at 4 AM, which I've asked her and my siblings not to, because it makes me think, immediately: they've been murdered. *How would we text you if we're dead?* Cartoon mothers do the most impossible ridiculous things, I say. Don't you know? My mom texts me at 4 AM to say, *I saw this thing today on Facebook and I'm gonna do it. We all need to leave (live). There's nothing for us here. There's nothing for anyone.*

What thing, mom?

EXPERT SERVICES

~~$129~~ **$50**

_________________ Submission________________

✓ 100% Guaranteed Entry to the Permanent Residency Visa program
✓ Full Assessment Report
✓ Eligibility Test
✓ Targeting to Improve your chances of immigrating

Payment Information

That's a scam, mom. That's not how it works. Please don't throw away your money. Your little, muscle ironing painfully earned money. You got that ad because, I don't know, your phone hears you say you're leaving this país de mierda all the time. Don't you know Facebook is the architect of targeted-ads? Don't you know it'll listen to your heart's wants and desires—treat it with the tenderness of a prayer always meant to be answered. They don't care if you're a cartoon as long as you have any money left to give them. It's all a scam, mom. Please don't try to make sense of it. Please don't give them any more of you. You're not a cartoon, mom. You're my mom. Why are you up at 4 AM—oh, yeah, it's 2 AM for you. Why are you up at 2 AM? Yes, I know. I know you're worried. I don't know if we'll get COVID again. Yes, I saw that. More rise in crime and poverty expected for next year. It makes sense, mom. Yes, of course I'm coming home soon, para la Navidad. I will bring you cartoon gifts—oversized unsquared boxes. I will bring you American-brand gifts. I will bring you

your body.

SAÚL HERNÁNDEZ

Sound of Myself

I.

I was ~~obsessively~~ jealous of parrots, how
they can mimic sound. Speak without

the weight words carry. Sometimes
I dream of digging my fingers into

the beak of a parrot, splitting it open.
Searching for all the sounds

it has ever heard. At the library
I undo what's beneath my tongue,

whisper to the dictionary:

        Am I   Am I   Am I—

II.

Not everything you do needs a word,
Amá says drying my body with a
fresh towel. I can smell the sun on it
from it being on the clothesline all day.

She wraps me in a yellow cobertor.
Her mouth slides words into existence,
Te ves mas mejor asi.

In the living room Apá throws back a beer while
gays fight for their rights on the news.
He takes a glimpse of me in yellow, squeezes the
beer can in his right hand, burps, spells out
with his yeast breath into the air:
Maricones pendejos.
I remove the blanket off me, drag it to my room.

The word
            maricón
                        not far
                                    behind me.

Everything I do needs a word.

III.

In college, I read Gertrude Stein,
a rose is a rose is a rose—
I unravel petals all day
with my tongue. I tease a boy,
tell him I don't like anything
going in me, unless it's love.
We laugh.

In the morning I ask him,
What would you call
what we did last night?
His answer: *We don't*
have to call it anything.

And he's right.

Unless   it's love unless it's love   unless—

IV.

As a child I once asked Amá:
Am I…

While wearing her blouse, covered in
yellow and blue regurgitation of flowers.

She opened her mouth to slaughter me.

V.

Sometimes in my dreams / I don't kill the parrot / it's free /
it flies high above / where there is no sound

just vibrations / waves of the wind
coming together / pushing into ears / never the mouth /

I wake up / find my mouth full of ellipses /
I need sounds / for where I am living

SAÚL HERNÁNDEZ

The Boy y el Hombre que se Comió el Relámpago

The sky of Salitrillos, MX flickered down on
Abuelo, young, driving his faded F-150
on unpaved roads, the sky groaned,
coughed lightning. He sped,
not wanting to be caught in the storm, his
whole body bobbed when he ran over rocks on the
road. Abuelo was too busy

holding the steering wheel to notice the sky burst
into shards of glass, a ball of
fire bouncing in his lap. When he saw it he said,
chinga su madre, tried to blow it out like candles
on a birthday cake, but it seemed to laugh.

He pulled over, opened to door ready to throw it out,
when he held the sphere he felt like he
was touching life for the first time. As he
gasped in disbelief, the ball of fire went inside

of him. Abuelo was found a day later by his
compadre passed out inside his troca. He went
down in his pueblo as el hombre que se comió
el relámpago.

The day I drove from El Paso to San Antonio
for winter break I got caught in a storm too.
The sky, one great mirror with clouds cracking,
if I took a glance at the sky one more time
I could break it, unleashing whatever was behind it.

When the sky broke down my windshield blurred,
I pulled over. I remembered Abuelo's story,
asked myself, if we inherit our ancestors' experiences,
if I have lightning inside of me.

When Amá's heart was struck by lightning
I remember she yelled Apá's name,
we found her in the kitchen, her whole body
bending and twisting, Apá holding her head,
aquí estoy, aquí estoy. Amá couldn't
hear him, she kept twitching. When the ambulance
arrived she was conscious, she didn't remember

what happened to her. After the stroke
Amá became a storm, her rage would last minutes
then as if nothing had happened. For years I have
wondered what broke inside her.

When my ex-boyfriend and I had late night talks on the
back of my GMC Sierra we would tell each other
stories of ourselves. I told him about my Abuelo.
He laughed so hard that night he said, *You're full
of shit.* I shrugged my shoulders then told him that's
why when I kiss you sparks fly. He said, *tell me*

something you've never told anyone before. I stayed
quiet for a bit then said, I wish I was light, to be
translucent, to be able to pass through someone's body.
He got on top of me that night, unzipped
my pants, leaned down to kiss me. *You don't
have to be light to pass through someone's body.*

The day Abuelo died, he was sitting outside smoking
his last cigarette, his hair damp from his shower,
his right leg crossed on his left leg, his shirt unbuttoned
halfway, so he could feel the night breeze, a Coca-Cola
glass bottle on the side of the chair. As he got up his right
arm twisted, fingers curled, his mouth clenched, his eyes

almost burst. He shouted for my Abuela, she called
for my tíos, their feet picked up dirt and debris as they
all carried my Abuelo's body into the back of the F-150
pick-up truck. They said his body looked like a relámpago
zigzagging uncontrollably.

Then Abuelo took one last breath,
all at once his whole body releasing
the electricity inside him.

When the storm passed, I looked up at the sky, thought of
how many things pass through clouds, of how it will be when
lightning comes out of me, will my body curve, braid itself into all my
ancestors and surrender to the sky.

KYLE OKEKE

The Monks of Abuja

There is something about having your eyes open but seeing nothing but blackness. Something that reminds you of everything you hate about yourself, or every embarrassing moment you've had. I still remember when Mama was beating me with a belt, and I was screaming I love you! to convince her to stop. I still remember the time I started praying after masturbating, then started smashing my head against the pillow of my bed for the next few minutes. I don't know if I believe in God or not; I guess that means I don't—but who wants to take a chance with eternal hellfire? I flick the lighter in my hand. I wave it around in the closet as if it were a firefly, then smother it under my fingertips. I've been waking up and going into the closet each morning, then by the time I get out the sun would already be down. Mama would look for me and sometimes and find me there, mad because she thought I had left the house and gone somewhere. I keep hiding in different closets of the mansion, each one with their own darkness.

We're in Nigeria in the city of Abuja at my family's mansion, and I'm hiding in closets because I now prefer to live in that silent blackness. I'm "vacationing" here because Papa had found gay porn on my phone and computer while snooping around. I was just curious, but no matter how hard I tried to tell him I wasn't gay, he wouldn't believe me. So, after a belting and prayers, he sent me with Mama to live in Nigeria with my grandmother on Mama's side for a month, and to spend my entire days in some Christian Pentecostal education class for troubled young boys. Papa had made me shave my head bald before coming here. The rest of the boys in the class had also been shaved bald too. They were all pretty weird, some young, and some older. My first day there, Mama had met Priest Ibekwe, the teacher, who was also bald, telling him what was wrong with me. The preacher's fingers squeezed my head as he started praying about God's direction, then he told me I would be born again. The next day, I was in the class, sitting on a chair with a torn red cushion so all the fluff was exposed, and the brown wallpaper of the room was also torn, exposing the wood of the building. I was surrounded by a bunch of other boys. Priest Ibekwe would be wearing a dashiki and white kufi cap and say Good morning everyone! God is with us! Amen? Then we'd all say, amen! There was one boy who'd scream it, his name was Chukwuma, who you could tell was clearly older than the rest of us by his patchy facial hair, and he sat next to me on my left. You could also tell by the way he talked and said amen that he was a bit off, he was the most enthusiastic. Most people avoided him because he was always rubbing against his groin with his hand, seemingly masturbating. I felt bad for him so I befriended him by giving him some cookies Mama had given me for lunch, and by letting him wear my glasses for a minute. Then there was a boy named Chibogu who sat on my right. I don't know why, but me and him just clicked. I felt like he was the only person there who was like me. I think it was because were both quiet and kept to ourselves, that we seemed to get along in our quietness. Me and Chibogu would play in the nearby woods during recess, and Chukwuma would follow us, smiling along with his tall and lanky self. One day, one of us had asked,

So, why are you guys here, and how old are you guys?

I'm here because I love God! Chukwuma shouted. I'm eighteen years old!

I'm here because I'm suicidal, Chibogu mumbled. I'm fourteen.

I told them I was there for both of those reasons, and that I'm fifteen.

I asked Chibogu, why are you suicidal?

I don't know. I just am, he says while examining a random stick. I'm just always sad. Some days I'm really sad. I don't feel like doing anything, I don't feel like there's a reason to do anything. One day I was upset about something my girlfriend said so me, so I had just walked into a busy street. All the cars swerved around me and each other and, can you believe it! None of them hit me! God must have saved me. They all danced around and stopped for me, I made them all stop, it was like I made the world stop.

Were you scared?

I was so scared.

Then why'd you do it?

I don't know.

What did your parents do after?

They beat me, Chibogu said while showing the faint marks on his leg. Then I told them I was going to do it again and again until I die, so now I go to this class.

Those marks are nothing! Chukwuma said. He takes off his shirt to show the belt marks on his back, where the skin was redder. They looked like tally marks made by someone who didn't know how to do tally marks. Lots of them going straight down or across and lots going diagonal.

Why'd you get beat so bad?

Because he was tugging his penis at some girls, Chibogu said.

No I was not! I was not tugging it at them! I was just looking at them! He lightly hits Chibogu's arm.

Then, a few weeks later, I had brought two silver lighters I had found in a cabinet while wandering the mansion (It's like a maze or a never-ending escherian stairwell. I decided that if I was going to be lost I might as well explore). We had played with the lighters in the woods, lighting leaves or sticks on fire then stomping them out. Me and Chibogu wouldn't let Chukwuma play with the lighters because we thought he might burn the whole place down, he couldn't even handle his bible without somehow mangling it. But he'd try and wrestle the lighters from us, he wouldn't even take cookies as a bargain. He would go, Please Please Please Please Please! Finally, I had told him to put his hand out. I lit the lighter and lightly burned him, then he went Owuouwouw! I said, see? This is dangerous, stay away, and gave him the rest of my cookies. But he already had something in his mouth. After some prying from me and Chibogu, we found out it was the key to where Priest Ibekwe kept all the wine for communion.

We just let him keep it. One time, we gathered a bunch of sticks and leaves and lit them on fire. It was a big, big fire. Then Chibogu said, watch this, and started peeing on it. Then so did me and Chukwuma. Then Chukwuma started masturbating. It made my curious, so I asked, who has the biggest penis? Then we all started tugging our penises, I had taken Chibogu's hand off his, and tugged his. He then did the same to me. I guess whatever Chukwuma had was contagious. I was so incredibly hot at that moment, I don't know why, but I couldn't stop sweating, I felt like the sun was God's eye focusing it's rays on me—and my breathing, it was like the air had increased in weight, I couldn't stand it. I had been staring at Chibogu while it was happening, and he was staring ahead towards the trees. A part of me was glad he didn't look back at me, I was scared of what would have happened if he did. In that moment, I started to dislike him. He reminded me of the reason I'm here in the first place, he reminded me of what I hated about myself. Once we were done, I saw something in the distance, it might've been a sign from God, there were these ants crawling all over a dead duck. I thought, what a horrible burial, and that maybe if the ants restrained their hunger, that duck could keep its beauty even in death. I thought, someone ought to kill those ants, the devil tempts them to ruin the beauty of things. I believed that God was telling me that temptation is like ants that crawl over you, tingling and itching your whole body, like what I had felt when I was touching Chibogu. I wondered if Priest Ibekwe was right, that I could bear that with enough prayer. But it never seems to be enough, and that angered me most.

Another day we went to a computer lab, if you could call it that. It was a row of like six computers outside with just a wall behind it and a roof over us. The three of us shared a computer with the few minutes we got. I looked up cicadas, because I thought they were especially loud in Nigeria. The hollow cicadas make the most noise, I find. Then they wanted to see pictures of America, so I showed them the Statue of Liberty. Then I looked up monks, because I had told Chibogu and Chukwuma that we kind of looked like them. They didn't know what they were, so I told them, monks are cool! I showed pictures of the burning monk who sat in the flames without moving, strong and unfazed.

A few days later, Chibogu said, what if I did what those monks did?

I wanna try! I wanna try!

Not you, Chukwuma. I have an idea. What if we take the wine from where Priest Ibekwe hides it, then I did what that monk did? Chukwuma was still sucking on that key.

(I knew that the monks had done some special training to be able to do that, and how they died after. But for some reason I just went along with Chibogu.)

To make the world stop again, I said. I think we should send a message like monks. I think we should test if you can bear those flames.

Won't that hurt a lot?

But the monk did it, right? Besides, I'll make sure to have a bucket of water with me if it goes bad, I reassured Chibogu. Chibogu thought again.

This would upset my girlfriend, I don't know if I want to die yet.

I don't want to die either!, Chukwuma shouted

Shut up Chukwuma. Chibogu, why don't you want to die? There's nothing good to hope for. You seem like you're always going to be sad no matter what. Besides, you won't die. Remember: God will not allow more than you can bear. Chibogu thought more, while examining a rock.

But if I do die, I hope I won't upset my girlfriend. My girlfriend likes me.

Your girlfriend pities you. Nobody really likes someone who's sad all the time.

Do you like me?

Not if you're going to be sad all the time. Sometimes you have to be mad.

Mad at what?

Everything. Priest Ibekwe, your parents, the sun, the clouds, the trees, the rocks, even yourself.

I am mad at myself. I hate myself, Chibogu mumbled.

I do too.

So do I! I hate myself too! Chukwuma shouted.

We were quiet for a while. The cicadas were loud.

But God loves me, Chukwuma says. So I love myself.

But you just said you hate yourself. I do both! I hate and love!

Chibogu had decided to do it. He said, I think God loves me too. Then we all started praying, God loves me! God loves me! Jumping around, then smacking sticks on the ground, rolling in the leaves, frothing, spasming, it was like a reverse exorcism; I was spinning so much I thought my head was twisting 360 degrees up and back and sideways, then we started acting like Priest Ibekwe when he prays, by the blood of the lamb ! by the blood of the lamb God ! I Pray I pray I pray I Pray healing healing healing healing ! Deliverance deliverance deliverance yes lord yes lord yes lord yes lord ! Have your way have your way have your way ! Then Chukwuma and Chibogu had started praying in Igbo, then even I did! I didn't know what I was saying, but I was saying something. I wanted to see if these prayers would work, if God would save Chibogu.

Then he did it. We snuck into the nearby church and took the wine from behind the altar. After drinking a bit of it, Chibogu poured it into a large vase and walked into the courtyard with it, while I grabbed another vase for the water. Chibogu was surrounded by the other boys while he said what I told him to: Watch And Witness! God Will Make Me Survive These Flames! God Loves Me! God Will Not Allow More Than You Can Bear! He dumped the vase of wine on himself. Chukwuma for some reason started screaming, Chibogu no! I said, Shut up! He said No, you shut up! So I pushed him inside the church and locked him in from the outside. Chibogu lit the lighter, engulfing his body in flames. All the other boys in the courtyard scattered, and so did Chibogu. I would've poured the water on him after about 10 seconds of him sitting with the flames, but he scrambled so hazardly that I could hardly catch him. He was the opposite of those monks, running and spinning and dashing around at something like the speed of light, wailing and crying. He would zip all around, a few other things catching fire, at some point he even flew. He was like a fly that went bzzzzzzzzzzz but instead screaming as he whizzed past, before collapsing in front of me—I don't even know how, he just appeared there out of some kind of blur. So I poured the water on him, and it made the fire erupt even more, and I ran a safe distance away. Maybe the bucket of water had been turned into wine, I don't know. The now arriving Priest Ibekwe with an extinguisher was able to kill the flames. I stayed after a while and watched the ambulance and adults come in and take him away. I tried to tell them that Chibogu had just suddenly lit himself on fire, but Chukwuma came busting out the door of the church, wobbling I think in some drunken haze. He told them everything, about how I had told Chibogu to try to be like monks, and then fell to the ground, passing out. I was now in trouble. I had to have a one-on-one conference with Priest Ibekwe to explain myself. So I told him that Chibogu wanted to send a message, and that I prayed to God that Chibogu would be immovable in flames like the monks. And I told him that, through God, anything is possible right? I told him, I had truly believed it. And what was his face? He just looked at me, I couldn't tell if he was concerned or disgusted. I did say sorry, and I was sorry. But I guess it didn't seem like I was, my face was straight and still as I looked into the priest's eyes. I told him, it wasn't entirely my fault, God could have saved Chibogu if he wanted to. Maybe he was meant to burn, or deserved it, or maybe God was doing him a favor by letting him die. I told him, God works in mysterious ways. I thought he wanted to hit me, hard. So I asked him, would a priest hit a faithful child and servant of God? He answered with a swift slap. It wasn't hard at all, I just looked back at him the same way after readjusting my glasses.

After beating me till my body had marked, Mama was stunned at the sight of what she had done. She wouldn't touch me at all after that. Mama had to pay the priest off so he wouldn't speak to authorities, and also paid a large sum to Chibogu's family for his funeral, and Chukwuma's family. Chukwuma had drank so much of the wine that he got alcohol poisoning and was put in the hospital. I don't know what happened to him.

Grandma had found me in her closet a few hours ago. I asked her why Nigerians were so religious. She said we were because white people had come here, colonized, and spread the word of God. Then I asked, why are we following the religion of our colonizers? She seemed stunned and said that I should go eat while she speaks to Mama.

Now I'm in the closet of Mama's room, she's arguing with Grandma about something in Igbo and I'm watching them through the tiny blinds of the closet. They're shouting, and maybe spitting, and their words sound rough and harsh, but everything sounds harsher in Igbo. Then my grandma takes off her shoes and starts beating my mother. It was a weird thing to see, Mama, guarding her face with her hands as Grandma uses her weight to push Mama on the bed, slapping her wherever she can with her shoe. I think they're arguing about me, I can tell when they do. Grandma would always say that it was Mama's fault that the devil got to me.

When Grandma is done, she leaves Mama by herself, sniffling. Her arm covering her eyes, she stays laying on her bed like that for a few hours, until turning off the light. A while later, she begins to murmur to herself. I take the lighter out of my pocket, and slowly open the closet door as to not make any noise. I flick the lighter. I see Mama kneeling, her hands clasped as she's on her knees and her head bobbing as she whispers something, and I think her eyes are shut tightly. I watch her for a minute, she breaks her clasped hands only to do the cross symbol by drawing it in the air with a single finger then continues whispering. I don't know what she's saying but something in me feels like it does. I've been angry for so long, but seeing Mama there, muttering to herself in darkness, I feel something sad. Not a crying kind of sad, but a silent and immeasurable one. The kind that feels like it will last your whole life.

I tiptoe towards the bible on the nightstand and take it, then leave the room. The house is dark, but by now I know my way through it. I use the lighter as a little guide, and head for the front door of the mansion. I walk past the giant portrait of Papa that hangs above a table with a vase at the center that holds plastic white flowers, the lighter illuminating his image. He's wearing a purple dashiki lined with gold going down the middle, on the sleeves, and at the bottom, and wearing a purple kufi with golden embroidery. I take three flowers from the vase, and go to the front door, Papa's eyes following. He's smiling in that photo, but I feel he might reach out with his cold fingers and wrap them around my neck.

I take a rock I find outside and write my name in the dirt. Chikaeze. Then, *Chibogu.* Then, *Chukwuma.* I think what I felt for Chibogu was love, if that's what you call that. Then why—why did I throw the vase of wine on his burning body? I think I know how Chibogu had felt when I asked him why he was suicidal. I think, we are all animals, aren't we? Do cicadas know that when they're screaming, they're screaming for sex? Did the ants think twice before consuming the duck? Could they possibly? Does Chukwuma know why he continues to masturbate even after the beatings? And hadn't God made us to bear any struggle? So why did God make Chukwuma? All he knows is the pleasure. There is something in nature that just makes animals do things. So how could Chibogu or I know? I think, there are things we don't know about ourselves. Chibogu was suicidal because he just was. And I threw the vase of wine on him because, I think, something against my will just made me love and hate him. And I think, there is something born out of that helplessness. Something that spreads like fire. Something that burns and burns and burns. I don't know if I am the trees or the fire; I must be both; I must be seeing it all burn down.

I light the bible on fire and put the three plastic flowers on top of it. The cicadas are screaming, I hope they find their lovers. Surely some will. I stomp out the flames of the bible, then throw it as hard as I can. I throw the lighter too. It's dark outside, and I will sit in this darkness for a while.

I'm going to hell. I know I am. I know Chibogu is in hell too. If I am so lucky, I will see him there and apologize—and, I think, we will be like the monks; I will be like them now—but, looking at the stars, each one seemingly little from afar but truthfully enormous balls of fire—imagine if they all fell as flaming monks and turned the earth to ash. God—I nearly scream at the glow of them all.

◆◆Z KENNEDY-LOPEZ◆◆◆◆◆◆

An American Apocalypse in Twenty (20) Scenes

Begin by asking the audience to silence, but not turn off, their phones. Advise that this production features targeted seating, and it is therefore important that members be positioned in the seat number listed on their tickets. The show may or may not include the potential for gunfire (simulated or otherwise), home invasions, theft, embarrassment, shame, and, in some cases, death. Sloppy transitions encouraged.

ACT 1

Curtains up on an empty proscenium.

1. A woman enters, sweeping. When a gunshot claps from offstage, she falls. A man enters, looks at her gently, then teases the broom from her loose grip. He gets in a few sweeps before he, too, is shot. A figure who is neither man nor woman enters, and upon seeing both the bodies, goes to kick the broom from the stage — but they are also shot. Long-haired children enter, but for some reason, the unseen assassin has no more bullets. [The clicking of the empty chamber needs to be audible through the entire theater.] ***Legal Addendum 1: If asked, will you insist that the casting choices were colorblind?***

2. The stage rotates to reveal the assassin slipping out a side door to the street, not looking both ways, and being mown down by a speeding car. [Donors give a lot of money to have someone placed in a Target Seat; use your budget accordingly. The assassin should look, smell, taste, and sound like an assassin.]

3. [Atmospheric] World War 3 breaks out, mostly in the expected places, but in some surprising locales. This thoughtful one-act geopolitical thriller examines the ramifications of a global war in a post-global world. The actors make lightning-fast quick changes to show the passing decades; the ones who live to old age still feel the war's repercussions, no matter how far they run.

4. [Indie] The devil appears from a trapdoor, center stage. Angels descend, suspended by ropes to the sound of trumpets and white finery. They proceed to play monkey in the middle. [The prop they toss back and forth should change with each performance. Make it resonant, but not heavy-handed. Continue until the devil wins, or until the devil takes off his mask and complains that his feet are tired.] The devil takes the prop home, then mimes sleeping, then mimes bathing, then mimes eating breakfast and going about his day.

5. A large cloth snake enters, stage right, held aloft by four actors in 90s tent revival garb.

The snake weaves and swirls, then tears open to reveal a woman. The four actors fall to the ground, and she looks out over the audience and mouths: *Help.*

6. Repeat Scene 5, only prior to snake's entrance, the four actors kidnap the audience member in Target Seat 1. [The actors should play the abduction as staged and part of the show. The mood should be primed, but calm.]

7. A woman climbs from the trap door and goes through the motions of gardening. She speaks silently to what are either hummingbirds or people passing by. The man she hasn't been waiting for for years finally arrives, entering the scene dramatically so that she'll see him when she looks up, but not otherwise making himself known. [The amount of time it takes for her to notice him should vary with each performance, but never is she glad to see him.] She backs away, mimes scrambling into a car, and rockets out the driveway in such a hurry that the mime-car she mime-drives goes *bump* over something—something big.

8. The snake enters again, stage right, carried by the same four actors. The cloth pulls apart to reveal the woman, and she dramatically play-faints in faux-terror. The four actors invite an audience member onstage to dramatically play-revive the woman. Before they reach the woman, the audience member is given a broom. [Do not use real bullets. Dispose of the body.] ***Legal Addendum 2: This is why the tickets cost so much: insurance is a nightmare. You wouldn't believe how much damage an audience member can do.***

INTERMISSION

9.   A playful scene-cum-intermission experience, during which guests may now use the restroom. Those who hold it will be rewarded with a short performance telling the behind-the-scenes story of the making of a different show. Word on the street was that you wanted to use the deep sea tank at the aquarium for a singing-mermaid rendition of *Hamlet* you'd been working on. The tank hadn't been scrubbed out in years and the aquarium wasn't sure it was worth keeping, but they bought whatever you were selling, believed your madcap promise that one last spectacle would raise enough money to stay in the black. Vary your performance as needed, and remember that this scene is a distraction.

     a.   *Legal Addendum 3: Items forbidden to mention during intermission (please note that this is vital to the success of Scene 20): Oprah; gifts; looking under seats; surprises; home invasions; disappearances, general and specific; near misses; going missing; people who have gone missing during shows; things going missing recently; things going bump in the night; things that seem out of place; the sensation upon entering a room of knowing that someone was there just moments before you; codes; cracking codes; cracking safes; safe places; memories of visiting grandparents; things you keep hidden; keeping your hands where I can see them*

     b.   A note on logistics: Once the audience members to be placed in the Target Seats have been confirmed, their incriminating items should be acquired as quickly as convenience allows. Questions to consider when selecting items of sufficient incrimination are "What else are you going to incorporate?" and "What else are you going to claim as yours?" Store the items securely offsite until an hour before curtain, at which point they must be placed in the two-day shipping bubblewrap foamcore packages that will be taped to the underside of the Target Seats, excepting Target Seat 1.

ACT 2

Curtains up on a chaotic scene: actors frozen mid-action. Lights up and they resume.

10. [Adlibbed, cacophonous] In the West Wing: everyone is play-yelling, even for throwaway lines. The tone is confused: are they mad, nervous, playful? The audience learns gradually that in the midst of World War 3, California has decided to become a nation unto itself, independent of the Greater Union. The doors are flung open and the secret service enters the theater. *Sir,* they say, *we have reason to believe one or more of the people in this room are Californian separatist agents who mean you bodily harm, and until such time as we can identify the infiltrators, we insist that no one be allowed in or out of the building until the end of the show.* In the control booth, the robocall system begins dialing audience members in alphabetical order. [After the show, those who followed directions and silenced their phones or sent the call to voicemail will be treated to a message that says: *As a valued constituent of the newly independent nation of California, we're here for you—and your opinion.* They will marvel at the immersive marketing of the experience. Inform the audience that they should tweet and post using a hashtag of your choosing.] When the room settles, the president play-yells that the Resilient 49 are willing to play both sides of the fence to prevent secession: World War 3 becomes e-, ex-, and in-ternal. Show how time passes, how the farms perish, how the prime ministers of Canada and the other places that are other acceptably easy to navigate if you are white and only speak English say, *Sorry, we're full,* and no one listens. In this scene, your subtitles or ASL interpreters should mirror the play-yelling. [If you've not been providing either, restart at Scene 1; we'll wait.]

11. [Discreetly] The snake from Act 1 enters again, stage right, carried by the same four actors. The cloth pulls apart to reveal Target Audience Member #1 (kidnapped in Scene 6). They are given a broom. Offstage: a sound [loud, smacking], followed by a thud [falling, heavy]. [What you do to make that sound doesn't matter; be creative. Follow the audience member's lead. They are now the star of the show. Provoke them if you have to, make something happen. ***Legal Addendum 4: Permitted. The spectacle to capital expense ratio must be maintained.*** When the scene reaches an appropriate end, escort Target Audience Member #1 offstage. Dispose of the body.]

12. An improvised scene.
    a. The prompt is: "A Good Man Is Hard to Find" but the Misfit is less misanthrope and more of lycanthrope. And he's hungry!
    b. The category is: facts vs feelings.
    c. The prop is: a stolen wooden leg.
    d. The question that must be asked is: *If asked, would you meet with James Baldwin in Georgia?* It must be posed in the form of a riddle. [Dispose of bodies as needed.]

13. A rooster, a bald eagle, a raven, a peacock, and a turkey play a high-stakes game of strip poker. They move with the pace of practiced burlesque performers, going a feather at a time, covering the stage with down. [The goal of this scene is to provoke nervous discomfort. Performers are encouraged to get weird and escalate.] ~~*Legal Addendum 5: Please clarify and/or is this required for artistic integrity of the work?*~~ *STET*

14. The assassin walks past the facade of a hardware store. He spins his head right round, baby, pacing and grumbling as he works up the nerve to enter. But all those brooms and mops and buckets and child-sized brooms and hell even brushes because if you think about it aren't brushes and sponges within the broom extended universe? The cleaning supplies freak his shit out and he runs the four blocks home, pulls the gun out from under his father's bed. He sits on the edge of the stage and delivers a star-making monologue with grit, this young fag acceptably butch for the show's duration, holding the pistol as though rapt in prayer. [He should engage the audience to the point that when he lifts the pistol, they forget if they are an audience or a community. Will they stop him? What will his community do when they find out what he's done? What systems are in place to keep him from therapy? How are we going to get all this onstage? Tune in at the same time next week to find out.]

15. The snake enters again, stage right, carried by the same four actors. When the cloth pulls apart, out falls a county fair. Out falls a monument. Out fall the skeletons from every holy space where the dead rest that's been torn up or paved over. Out fell everything swept into museums. Out will fall the sound of every breath used to remake myth. Out fallen power and erasure and money. Out, felons, come on out.

16. [With complex blocking] The devil watches the woman who mime-drove her mime-car over an assassin who may or may not be the same assassin as earlier. *It gets complicated,* the devil monologues, *when you accept that time is less one long thread of cotton-polyester blend than an entire hoodie, and no matter where it touches your skin, you're in contact with strands pulling in multiple directions.* When the woman notices, the devil says, *Do I get points for accidents?*

17. An improvised scene.
    a. The prompt is: A gaggle of young refugees, brown and smudged in Post-War California, discussing whether gender even had a chance.
    b. The category is: the myth of American exceptionalism.
    c. The prop is: A packets of seeds and a dog who seems okay for now but who keeps exhibiting more worrisome behavior.
    d. The question that must be asked is: *Are there any walls left to break?* It should be unclear whether it is meant rhetorically.

18. The snake enters again, stage right, carried by the same four actors, only this is a real snake, and a big one too, not an easy-break cloth imitation used in abductions, so call it what you will, when all is said and done, the bottom line is when the chips fall where

they may, the creature doesn't cooperate. [As much as possible, ensure that this is so, but the devil is adamant that the snake must not be harmed.]

19.   The stage rotates to reveal the audience members who've been watching the show from the lobby, since the auditorium is only accessible by stairs and They "weren't able" to accommodate. Sure, They scramble to replace the monitors and tinny speakers with the real thing, but at this point it's too late, it's too much a spectacle. The stage rotates to a ramp-filled world. The stage rotates to dizziness, rotates to dissolution, rotates to remaking, rotates.

20.   The audience is directed to look under their seats, where randomly selected members will find taped the two-day shipping bubblewrap foamcore packages containing the incriminating items for the Target Audience Members. Confusion ensues as do denials because surely, if one found oneself suddenly and without warning holding a KKK robe, a stack of Kodakaroids of children in inappropriate positions and contexts, or something similarly damning—surely one would deny that these objects were one's. But who else is there to claim them? What would drive a theater to cast aspersions so? ***Legal Addendum 6: Could this be construed as slander, ambient or otherwise?*** [Pandemonium, if achievable, is encouraged. ***Legal Addendum 7: Technically, the secret service still has jurisdiction and is authorized per above to interpret and maintain that as they see fit until end of show.*** Eventually:] *Wait*, a voice calls out. The devil appears onstage beside a smoking brazier, flanked by the assassin, the angels, the four actors in 90s tent revival garb, the birds, the Oval Office, and the woman with the mime car. *I have a proposition*, the devil says, *if you'd care to hear?*

a.   If the audience does not care to hear: proceed to Scene 20c.

b.   If the audience does care to hear, the devil reveals that the owner of each incriminating item is among the audience. Either the owners each place their item in the brazier and set it alight while saying *Hail Satan*, or, if the audience votes with total unanimity, the devil will incinerate the items' respective owners. However, if the vote is not unanimous the souls of the audience are collectively forfeit. ***Legal Addendum 8: True?*** The devil, checking their phone, says, *We have 45 minutes until They kick us out of the building, but you have 90 seconds to decide.* [Allow the audience time to respond. However, proceed immediately to Scene 20c if they show signs of reaching consensus or if the Target Audience Members do as instructed. Also proceed to Scene 20c if at 90 seconds the audience has not reached a decision.]

c.   [Sloshy, acidic, thick with plastic fog and six-pack rings] The Ocean enters and drowns the whole fucking theater. [Exeunt all, except those who are left. Rinse and repeat until the concept of audience runs clear in the shower. The rest of whatever's bound to happen happens, and while we regret to show our hand so plainly at so late a stage, we feel it our duty to inform you that the question we've hope to leave you with is this: How silent is it all really, when there's no one left to hear?]

DANI PUTNEY

Track: "Dead of Night" by Orville Peck (2019)

Sparkle cowboy, flower rider,
horseback lover—
    shoot me saloon-style
in Virginia City, roll my corpse
      down Geiger Grade.
Just kiss me first,
  say *Country ain't your grandad's West.*
Tongue my hollow, I want to feel spikes
  rip my palate: *Country is fag land.*
    You're the daddy I've dreamt of,
the denim I love to press
  into my thighs. Your spur
licked my neck twice last week. I woke up
  dead each time.   The desert repeats,
see? Your fringe is the last sight
  I want to remember. But let's leave us
    a mystery—
      ride to Carson City at midnight,
  I promise to haunt the pony
tattooed on your bicep.

Hungerpressed

ya'll know it
or you never
sung supper-songs tapped on
can tops loosening binds
pried wide outdated soup & fruit
too hunger-sloshed
to be thankful enuf
for gaslit freedom from
[   ] & them.

sure of grace & grit
& gather i'd rather lay in
dim lit squats sans heat
than be splayed below blue-sky canopies
in fields touching down on green-gold touching
clouds & repeatedly ambered assurances
hush hush this this here
this here's what beauty's'posed'ta'be
touching down in every wrong way

no-no no no-homo home is home
home is conjured from bills overdue
blackouts & thrift store knock off Timbs
brown suede & drum set & never too cold
to jam to dance that's where magic sits
& everything less-valued left
in dumpsters after the raccoons get in

there in the late night stench
watch mama possum drag her coat
through plastic nets & littered tops
she's on a hunt for feed
her babies in a nearby brush will feast
from sticky delivery-gone-goo
soaking front paws in evening creams of grime
til satedly slumped against her lustred gut

mama midnight possum not my mama
poses caught off guard but fierce
stays her course & stares me down
she's the best looker mama who ever looked
at me & in her eyes i can do more
than bastard these humid nights

NEFERTITI ASANTI

the present is an adolescent wit 3 wishes

i'm rubbin & rubbin & rubbin my tummy
like it's a magic lamp like a swole blue
genie finna uncurl in a smoke trail clear
out my vagina & lay 3 wishes on me   i'd wish
for a new tummy less swollen wit not-babies
not flat neither   i could set it down on my side
table   soft & doughy like the memory
foam pillow at my back proppin me up so i can
swallow oatmeal still warm in my mouth
maybe a 2nd wish would be a 2nd mouth
on the quickest side of my cheek smilin when i am not
smilin spittin like a real monster would spit
on doctors that don't know what the freak they doin

i most love me when i'm dippin my fingers
in the paint i make each month   vermillion
when i say it   feel like
i got caterpillars crawlin between my teeth
swear they buildin cocoons i am careful
not to chew & swallow them too
pills water oatmeal tongue eddy in my mouth
my 2nd mouth recites picture book poems
in the silence between procedures
i ain't bled in such a long time i miss it

when my butterfly baby comes out
her cocoon i make my 3rd wish that bb
taps her little feet on my nose   kiss
my 2nd mouth then flutter away
to a good mommy who voice make dandelions
dance in a land where you don't need wishes
i say *vermillion*   my blood would come
like silk   doobie wrap me in a sailor moon cocoon
so no one not even god could touch me

NEFERTITI ASANTI

i have always had my hands

even when there was no field, no heads, no feathered things
to tend. had hands that knew tender swelled in front of the throat
when neck give reach   sunnin itself,   drinkin
up the light. dancin hands take a fistful of skirt & lift & lift & liiiiift
high-steppin over newly planted tomatoes, corn or like if i squat
over an unfamiliar plot i'll push   out   a funny-lookin seed & will
a thing to grow & grow whether or not i take myself past
the mason-dixon without that seed.   i still got hands

grateful to hold open a door for a pretty sateen thing passin thru
my eyes smile at the ground hopin a mistake will grow into a future
where my hand rests on the small of that passin thru pretty thing's back
& her lips touch the lip of the wine glass my lip touched & the clean
of the glass shine in competition with the shine of my teeth. half moon
in my mouth ain't too shy to present its tell-tale self here: we do not shake
hands like wrestin hangin fruit from the good neighbor's tree.

when these hands slow strangled the long neck of a used bass, the sound
come out never came out   again the music changed mostly changed me,
gave me round breasts anybody could mistake for clementines, gave me
lips too full to fit on my face   only   so it found another & another,
gave me eyes too squintin-narrow to never not seem suspicious of kids
sittin too-too quiet in the back of the class or a man scuffed everywhere
but his shoes ~~or a river warmer than the air above it~~. the music changed
[my] hands, made it so my fist could fit into a swallow's mouth clench,
unclench without breakin the beak.

GWENDOLEN AUBE

if you insist on being a girl

if you insist on being a girl
the best way is to be a girl
curled up inside an apricot

inside an apricot there are no
wolves, or dogs, or even baby dogs

yes there are geese, but they are kind
and do not bother much with their teeth
and they drink all their nutrients through straws

outside of apricots there are things
that are bad for girls like tsunamis
and very fancy televised dog shows

in these shows the dogs wear very pretty clothes
and sit pretty also, but these are not nice dogs
because they are quite stuck-up and their teeth
are stuck up, also

in an apricot you will have a small book to read
(i suggest "the masker" by torrey peters)
you can read that book a lot of times in an apricot

yes, if you insist on being a girl
you should be inside an apricot
where you are the stone
a waiting tree

& one day dogs will bark up you and piss on you
& you will have a million bugs on you
& your leaves will shake gently in the wind

& people who have just got glasses
after a long time of not having glasses
will look at you and say
                    "oh,
I can't believe I've missed this"

TARIK DOBBS

from Henry Ford's Sociological Department

Company English School Yearbook Sorted by Ethnicity

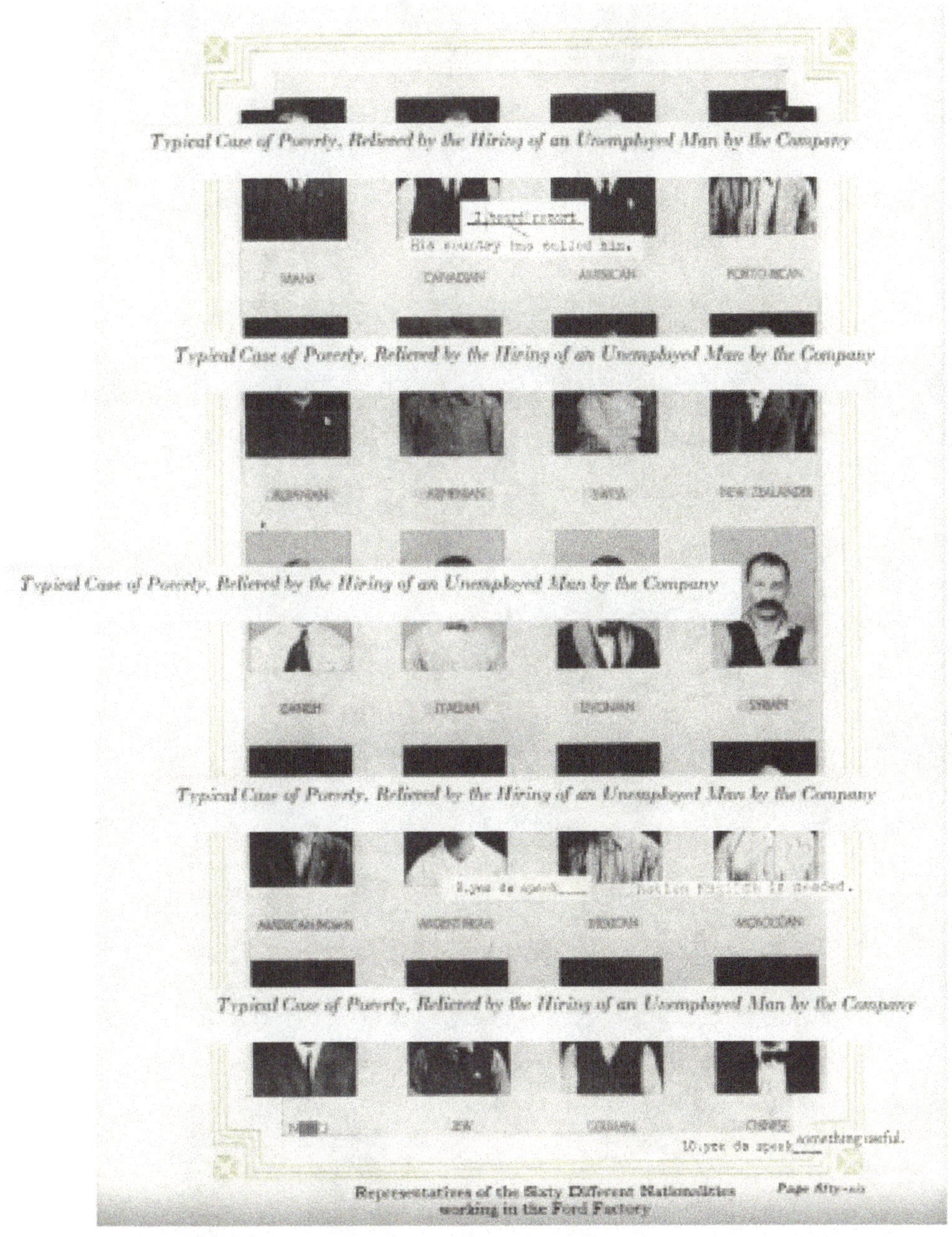

from *The Henry Ford Archive, Dearborn, MI*

An Agent Writes, Education Will Do More Lasting Good than Stove Polish for this Kitchen

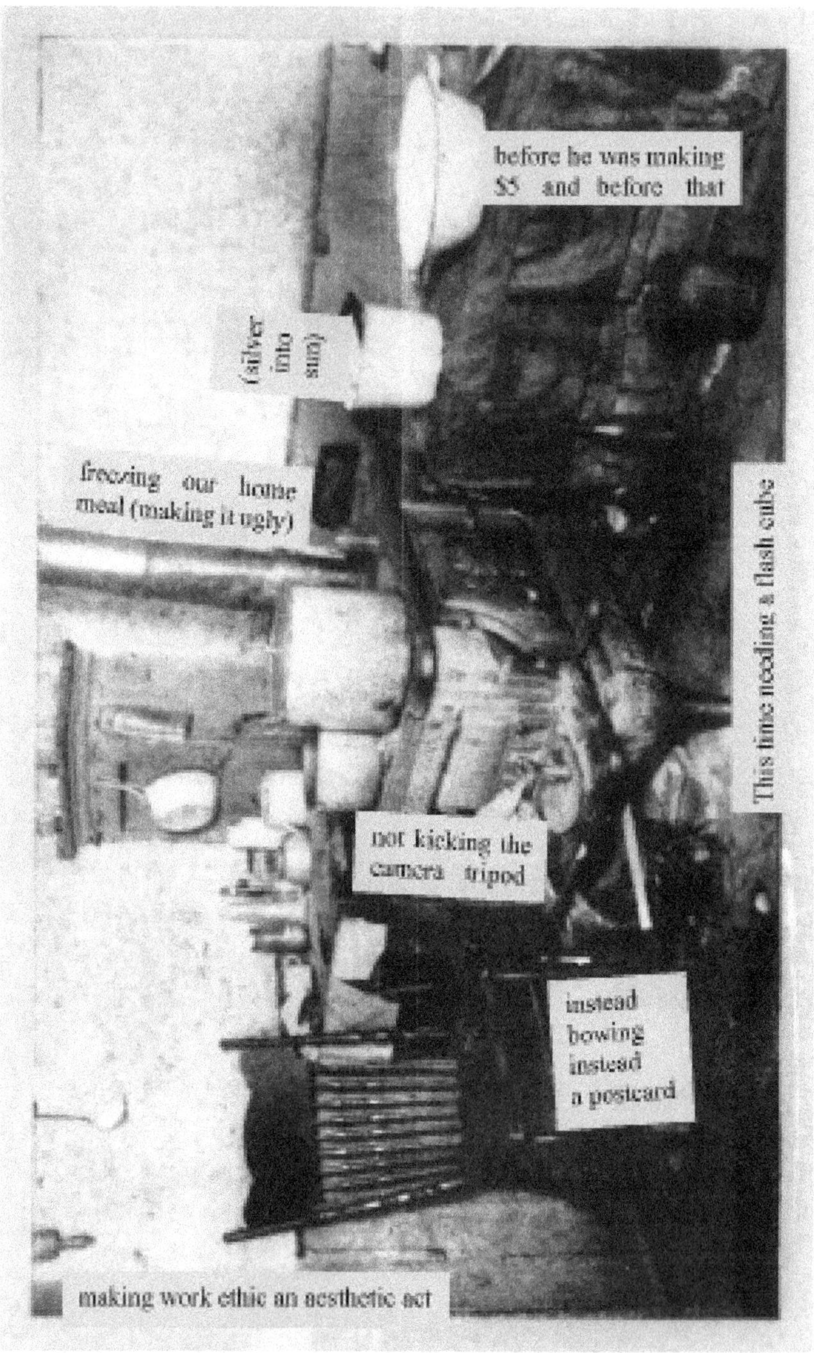

from The Henry Ford Archive, Dearborn, MI

Ford Agents Clear an Employee's Yard, 1914 // Henry Ford Draws his Birthplace, 1913

from The Henry Ford Archive, Dearborn, MI

Kitchen Improvements Upon a Company Agent's Second Inspection

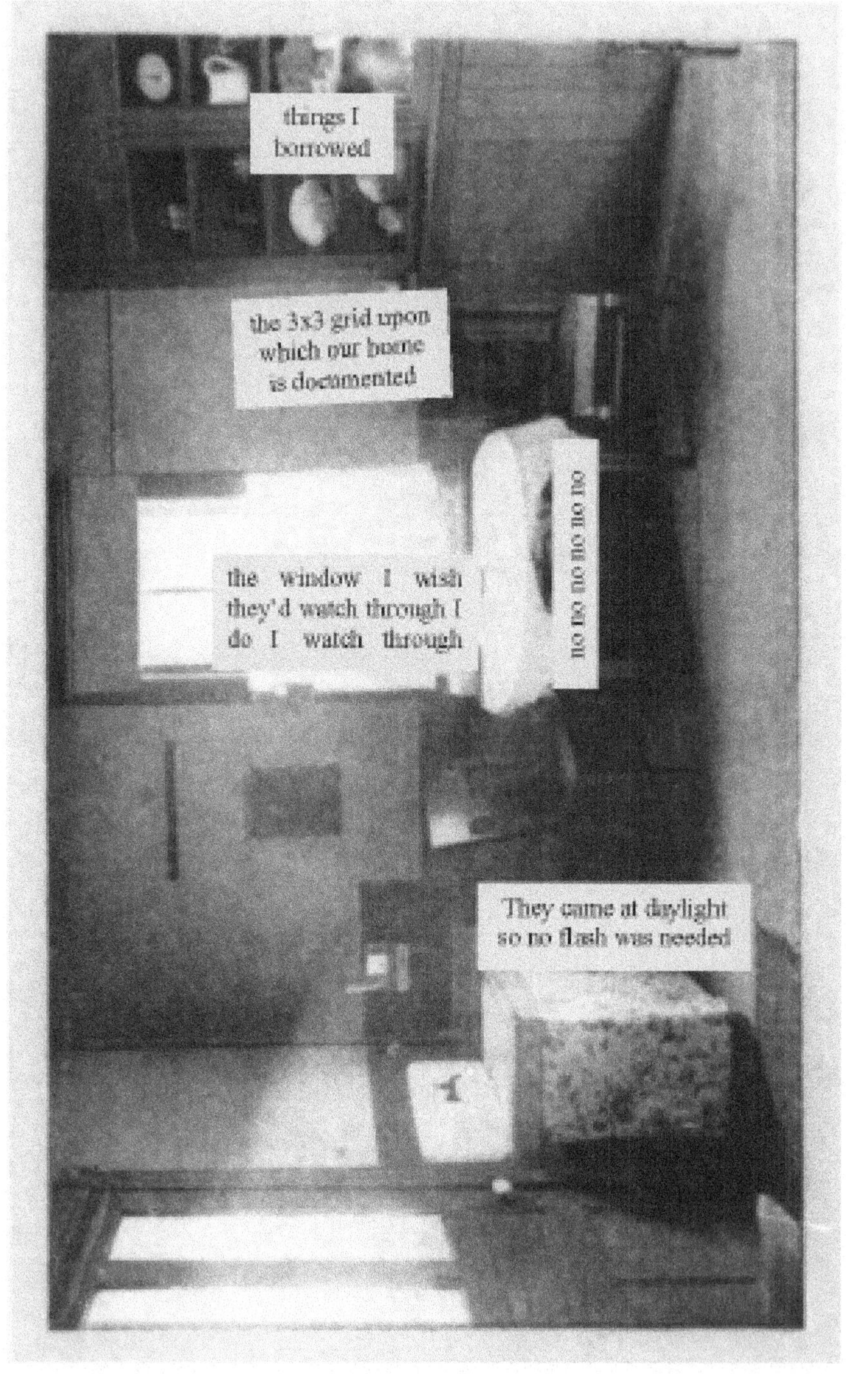

from The Henry Ford Archive, Dearborn, MI

Advertisement by Ford Company, or What a Human Can Do

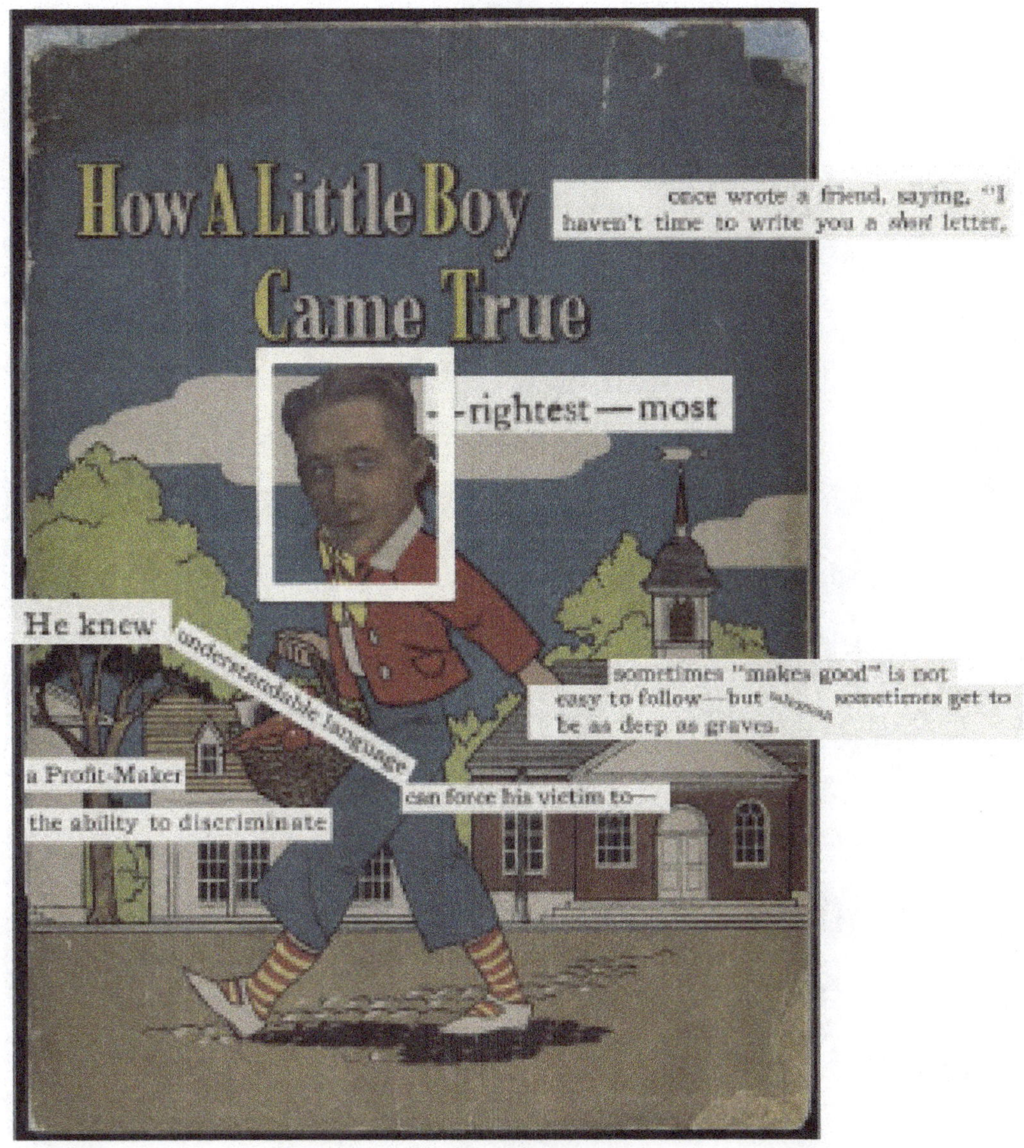

from The Henry Ford Archive, Dearborn, MI

Representative Home of Ford Employee at Time of Second Investigation

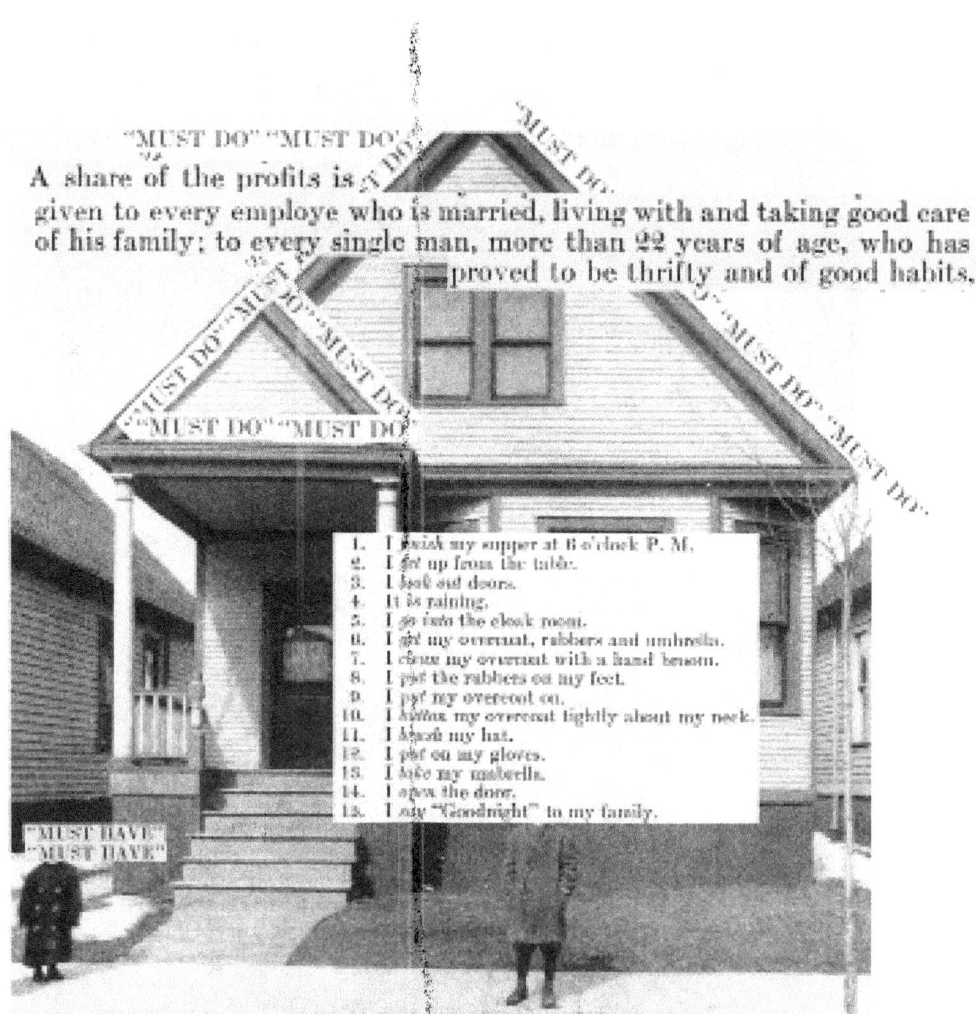

from The Henry Ford Archive, Dearborn, MI

Something Useful

Self-Determination

Our Liberty Pole May-Day, 1892, by the Company Cartoonist

from *The Henry Ford Archive, Dearborn, MI*

ÀKPÀ ÁRINZÈCHUKWU

Missing 23-Years-Old Man, Abakaliki

Have you seen our son, pearl blossom—
in whose eyes the fires of hell & heaven converge?

He was last seen at Brackenbury's, a bird in water.
If he isn't singing about the moon, he is the moon.

& when he is not the moon, our son pretends to be the ghost
of every man who died without living in the warmth of a lover.

The moon when it fades, our son is a thousand-year depression.
Look at these tight pantaloons, admit you've never seen such an impossible

world. Our family, world of our own. We shrapnel towards a fitting dress but
end up a loose gown.

If you've seen our son, he is a thousand-years-old impossible rock. The sun
sets on his face while the morning is still young, an igneous weathering

into storm. Our son, stout, God's fury, storms into darkness & it is more darkness.
He is one darkness & a thunderstorm's possible. Look at God, isn't he a wonder?

In one breath he created happiness & in another, man as a synonym of sadness,
shards of self-loathing. It still goes that a man bereft of love is a landmine,

self-destructing towards hunger. If found, God, fill in a man desires to grow
wings, & fly towards Islam. Peace that comes from loving & being loved.

Have we but anymore regrets left in our wallet, we'd buy a man sunshine,
lots of rays, a horizon, then a truck to drive far beyond into aurora.

ÀKPÀ ÁRINZÈCHUKWU

Almanbudh/Castaway

Loneliness is not the absence of light.
Maybe, it is a cat. It takes what it's given,
goes after the sun still, chasing
its shadow through the city till it catches
the melancholic hands of darkness,
clawing & gnawing at them till
what was once a moment becomes
the language of the loneliest creatures.
I did what has to be done. Like every
good son I wheeled the sun down
into the ocean. Rid of this heat now,
mum, look at me, cleaner than our past.
I am twenty three years & five nights in & out
of your womb & my sweetest thing is when
I can love no more boy but you. My sweetest
thing is when I am neither your sin nor mine
nor anyone's. The virus has gone underground,
mother, won't you open the door & pray with me?

Honora Ankong

Discussing Depression with My Mother

Because somewhere on my journey across Atlantic

I lost my tongue—I have negotiated silence

as ailment for migrant pain. In my new country,

I am tangled in bed with a woman and when we kiss,

she shoves a new tongue in my mouth. The woman

in my bed asks to touch me where it hurts the most.

I bring her hand to a map—all my pain is country-

shaped. On a phone call, my mother

and I take turns naming our losses. I attempt to put language

to what I am absent of   but the language on my tongue

is that of an empire. When I forgot my mother tongue

I further exiled myself from my homeland. I tell my mother

that I am carrying a black   hole in my chest.

She says, *I know, I tendered its dark.* My mother is also the mother

of my depression   meaning she was present at its nativity.

My old country is a jealous god, so when I worship at the altar

of America I get punished. My mother cooks peppersoup and sets

some aside as offering but our gods are hungry for elegies.

My mother regrets bringing me to America—

says, *this country is where love comes to die.*

MOLLY McCLOY

Tarzan and the Rabbit

My two brothers and I just didn't understand the kids who got all bent out of shape about their parents' divorces. By the time I was twelve, and my mom kicked my dad out, the three of us had been lobbying for his exile for at least three years. If you'd asked me back then what I thought of my father, I would have said, "That guy? Total dick."

I'd had enough of his ridiculous rages; he'd scream at me for a full 20 minutes if a bath towel was not folded properly or respond to the F on my older brother Tom's ninth-grade report card by pushing him up against the wall and berating him, drill sergeant-style. Shortly after my family moved to our new house in the Phoenix suburbs, we sent my dad back to live in our old house in the city. My parents legally separated.

It was the summer of 1982, and our new house had a private bedroom for each of us, and a pool. My mom went back to work as a nurse and bought us the microwave and the VCR my dad would never spring for. She went out on Fridays with her nurse friends and got looped on strawberry daiquiris.

For the first few weeks it was refreshing to see my 36-year-old mom having so much innocent fun with this pack of lightweight Happy Hour gigglers. When one of the "girls" held a "Tupperware" party and Mom left for the party dressed in her standard Cherokee stretch-waistband-jeans and puffy-aerobics-shoes-and-koala-bear-sweatshirt outfit, I imagined them all gathered in some gal's living room, drinking pink wine out of plastic cups and pawing through piles of juice pitchers and cereal bowls. I had no idea what they were really up to.

"I ordered the big one. Do you think I should have gotten a smaller one? What type of batteries does it take?" I heard Mom ask a friend on the phone after the party. She giggled and, when she saw me watching her, she stretched the phone cord around the doorway into her room and then giggled more from behind the door. Her laughter took on this familiar and disturbing lilt as I realized this was the same type of high-pitched hooting she'd made a few months prior when she'd paged through her gag birthday gift, *Buns*, a photography book full of close-up shots of male models' asses. A few days after the phone call, the "Tupperware" my mom ordered arrived on our doorstep, a long narrow box like one that might hold a pair of drumsticks, and I knew it was not a salad spinner or a melon-baller. I didn't want to know what it was.

Usually after my mom left for work at 2 PM, my 11-year-old brother Jake would hop on the handlebars of my bike and we'd ride out to my friend Anna's apartment in the desert foothills on the edge of town. Anna was a tough 13-year-old I'd met on the junior-high basketball team. She had dark, straight, shoulder-length hair and cracked her knuckles a lot, an act which always made me notice that her hands were huge and nearly as strong as a man's. Anna's mom was always on some mysterious trip to Reno, leaving behind a pair of pony-tailed and paunchy bikers to look out for Anna—harmless men in leather vests and bandanas who slouched on the couch while we picked the seeds out of their marijuana for them.

After smoking the pinch of weed the bikers gave us as payment for the seed-picking chore, Anna, Jake, and I would blast AC/DC and Judas Priest from the living room stereo. "Breaking the law, breaking the law," Rob Halford shrieked on the cassette tape while we wrestled and turned somersaults on the shag carpet, happily stoned and nostalgic for our elementary school days, a time before we walked the halls at Royal Palm Junior High dressed in black concert T-shirts, pretending not to hear the rich kids who called us "Rocker losers." "Your mom shops at K-Mart," they'd taunt. "Your dad works at McDonald's."

Jake and I were high and filling up the bong in Anna's bathroom sink one time when we noticed a long, narrow box—like one that might hold a pair of drumsticks—sitting on the back of the toilet tank. The label read "Tarzan."

I picked up the box and tried to peer through its tiny cellophane windows, but Jake grabbed it away from me before I could see anything. He held the box at arm's length and then gingerly pried open one end, letting Tarzan fall onto the bathroom floor with a soft thud and a slight bounce. Contrasted against the vinyl of the yellow floor, the object looked all the more shocking: a black shaft of solid rubber about twelve inches long, a realistic-looking penile head on one end, and at the other end…another head. "Dude!" Jake called out to Anna. "Dude, your mom has a double-dildo! It's got two ends. We all know what *that* means."

Anna came into the bathroom and stared at her mother's dildo on the floor. A good friend would have comforted her in her moment of painful vulnerability. But I was too disturbed and embarrassed to respond well, my head filled with images of Anna's mom naked with another woman, Tarzan swinging between them. This was a time in my life when I didn't want other kids to look at my own mom at all, even if she was wearing a koala bear sweatshirt.

Jake and I both freaked out and tried to distance ourselves from Anna's embarrassment. And then we turned on her. Jake and I already teased Anna regularly about her mom's trips to Reno. Since Anna's mom always came back with big wads of cash, we decided this meant she was a prostitute. Now, as we stood there in the bathroom and Jake handed Anna the box with Tarzan in it, our friend's mom was suddenly a lesbian prostitute. For weeks, we were merciless about it. "Can I have a sip of your Coke?" Anna would ask. We'd reply, "No, dude, your mom's a gay hooker. No way."

My mom, who couldn't figure out why we were suddenly torturing Anna all the time, asked us, "Do you keep her around just to make fun of her? With all those jerks at school, you should at least be nice to your only friend."

Anna tried to remain stoic and wait out our latest wave of teasing, but, unfortunately for her, Doublemint Gum commercials aired hourly on TV in those days, with these bikini-clad twins singing the jingle, "Double your pleasure, double your fun." One Thursday afternoon when we were all sitting on our couch watching a Gilligan's Island rerun, Anna finally cracked. The twins sang, Jake smirked, and Anna lunged at him. Jake leapt over the coffee table; Anna stepped on the couch and launched over the table to tackle him in the middle of the living room floor.

My mom came out of her room just as Anna caught Jake in a chokehold, his neck firmly clamped between the forearm and bicep of her right arm. Jake said, "Your mom's double-dicking it with another chick." Anna retaliated with, "So what? Your mom has one. She has The Rabbit."

Oh no. I knew right then that when I wasn't around, my brother and my friend had somehow found my mom's long, narrow package. The two of them knew what was in it—this mysterious "Rabbit"—and now my mom knew that they knew.

Mom had to think fast. She had to do something about us three kids who had been stomping all over the furniture and choking each other, the hooligans who had gone into her closet and raided her privacy. If my dad had been there, he would have screamed and kicked and broken something. He would have sent my friend home and assigned us kids time-consuming outdoor chores so he could have the TV and La-Z-Boy to himself. But now my mom had to handle us on her own. Her eyes narrowed and her chin jutted out in a posture of challenge and defiance. "Do you want to see it?" she asked. "I'll show you."

What happened next is the "most embarrassing moment" I could never cite when asked by an innocent date or a circle of co-workers in an icebreaker session. It was all too hard to explain. My mom as a sexual being. My mom as a sexual being in front of her kids.

The brand-new toy was out of its box, stripped of its plastic wrap, and in her hands before I could stop her. It whirred around and around, a seven-inch pink rubber shaft rotating clumsily. Affixed to the shaft like a low-slung saguaro branch was the cute little rabbit head, its ears vibrating in a mad amphetamine twitch. Around and around, it whirred, a new gadget like the microwave and the VCR. I winced, shut my eyes tight, but I could still see it in my head, rotating. It was as if The Rabbit were emitting life lessons from my mom. In my imaginings, the slowly rotating shaft conveyed its morals in a low, hesitant baritone like Forrest Gump: "Be nicer to your friends. Guard their vulnerability as if it were your own." The twitchy rabbit ears tapped out a frantic, high-pitched Morse code: "Respect-your-mother's-privacy!"

I would never, ever tell kids at school about Tarzan, and Anna would not tell them about The Rabbit. My mom's shock effect worked—it got my brother out of Anna's chokehold and made Anna feel better about her own home life. Around and around went The Rabbit, and soon all of us were laughing—Anna laughing at me, Jake and I laughing because we didn't know what else to do, Mom laughing more softly as the embarrassment started to kick in. Around and around went my mother's phallus, the disciplinary head of the household, a way better dick than my dad.

MAR STRATFORD

Passion Play

Is it a coke situation or a coke problem Cassie asks Ricky. One thing I like about Cassie is she's always got a smart way of putting things. If she asked me, I would tell her that I have an alcohol situation and a student loan situation and a Jesus situation, but I don't have any problems. Ricky touches the rivulet of blood spilling from his nostril. It's all cool he says. Cool cool cool. His voice sounds like a podcast at 1.5 speed.

Then fix your make-up, get ready. We're on in ten.

Cassie is Roman Soldier 1 and Ricky is Longinus. Ricky is paid more than any of the Roman Soldiers, but Cassie has worked at the Ozark Mountains Passion Play longer than anyone, so people listen to her. Ricky goes to the dressing room to fix his make-up. Roman Soldier 2 watches a soccer game on his phone. Roman Soldier 4 asks me if I'm going to eat the rest of my fries. I say no, you can have them. I'm Roman Soldier 3. If the Roman Soldiers were a boy band, I would be the Hot One. But we aren't a boy band, we're washed up bit part actors. Also, out of everyone in the Ozark Mountains Passion Play cast, Jesus is the Hot One.

Center stage, Jesus hangs from the crucifix. The spotlights hit him dead on highlighting every muscle on his bare torso. He's like a fucking Michaelangelo sculpture, this guy. Long dark hair, big compassionate eyes, muscled yet slim, the ability to shed a single tear on cue. The old Jesus, who couldn't weep on stage at all, quit last year to move to Las Vegas. We closed for a week. When we reopened, Carlos had cast this guy, the new Jesus. I heard Carlos poached him from an off-off-off Broadway production of *Jesus Christ Super Star*. Now, Carlos says, profits are soaring, thanks to all the photo package sales.

Jesus flutters his eyes shut. A single tear trickles down his cheek. Beneath the leather skirt of my costume, my dick is rock hard. Up in the booth, the sound guy plays a gong. That's Longinus's cue. He doesn't move. I elbow him and he jumps backwards like he's been electrocuted, into a three-tier display of areca palms. The plants crash to the floor, spilling dirt everywhere. Fuck fuck fuck we all hear Longinus say before the audio guy mutes his lapel mic. The light guy does what he can, and we cut to a full stage black-out.

In the dressing room, I scrub make-up off my face and change into loafers, khakis, and a t-shirt with the Ozark Mountain Passion Play logo. The crowd's cheer hits my ears like a tidal wave, letting me know that, despite the botched crucifixion, Jesus has risen from the dead. Every matinee, every evening show, the crowd cheers like that—desperately relieved—as if there could be any other outcome. They're extra loud today, a bigger audience than usual, because it's Holy Thursday. Three days until we get our Easter bonus. I go to put fresh batteries in the Polaroids.

In the hallway outside the utility closet, Carlos is whisper-yelling at Ricky. Ricky's coke situation has turned into a coke problem. This is a family-friendly business Carlos hisses. Ricky hands over his helmet and sets down his spear like a war-weary member of an out-maneuvered phalanx. I feel bad for the guy. But also, this means one of us is in line for a promotion.

After the show, Carlos's assistant gets the audience lined up in the theater lobby. The Weeping Women snap photos, and the Roman Soldiers handle the cash. You can get your picture with Mary, Mary Magdalene, John the Apostle, or Jesus. Everyone wants a picture with Jesus.

Jesus is like no problem. He puts his arm around women who gaze at him like he's the real deal. He shakes hands with the men who would be too embarrassed to show this much affection to any other male. He cradles little babies, even the screaming ones. He pats their backs and their tiny red faces unscrunch into a smile and all the women coo.

I bet you wish he would hold you like that Cassie whispers to me. Cassie is a huge butch dyke who clocked me the day we met. I whisper shut the fuck up. You should talk to him tonight Cassie replies. Jason's a sweet guy. You could be friends.

I don't want to be friends I say. I want to suck him off. Then, what do you mean, tonight? Did you invite him to the bar? The Roman Soldiers have a tradition of getting shitfaced every night during Holy Week.

Cassie looks shifty. Maybe, she says. He probably won't show, anyway. Jason's too classy for McCarthy's.

A man in khakis and a polo hands me a fifty. I make change for his $29.99 photo package. God bless, I say. He thanks me and walks away. I turn back to Cassie. Did you hear Ricky got fired?

By the time we are closing for the night, everyone has heard that Ricky got fired. His locker hangs open, empty of personal belongings. Roman Soldier 2 picks up the spear, raises it above his head.

How do I look?

Like a dipshit Roman Soldier 4 answers.

Roman Soldier 2 puts down the spear, shoves Roman Soldier 4, gets shoved back, and they're on the floor, four arms and four legs scuffling around like an insect on its back. I don't think either of them get a good swing in before Cassie and Judas pull them apart.

Judas asks what the hell is your problem but I get it. I'm just like them: a resume of starring roles from all four years of high school, a BA in theater from a small Southern college. Henry Higgens, Captain Von Trapp, Hamlet, Oberon, I played them all. This part, Roman Soldier 3, this was supposed to be temporary, I was supposed to hang out here for a few weeks, impress Carlos, get recast. When Old Jesus left, that was my chance. But no. Now, Longinus is up for grabs, and if I don't get the part, this situation, this little shitty job situation, is going to become a goddamn problem.

I tell Cassie I'm skipping drinks tonight. The Roman Soldier bonhomie is suspended until Longinus is re-cast. In the corner, Jesus laces up his sneakers. He has AirPods in, oblivious to the rest of us. He is probably the only person in this show without any problems or even a situation. He is so fucking perfect.

My car is doing this thing where the engine overheats if I go above 30 but I've been waiting for the Easter bonus to get it fixed. Apparently I've waited too long, because tonight when I leave the theater, I turn on the ignition and thick black smoke comes pouring out the hood. I get out, pop the hood, push my sleeves up, and stand there, smoke stinging my eyes, like I know what I'm doing. Cassie would probably actually know what to do, but she's already gone.

Car trouble? Jesus asks. I look up. He comes over, stands next to me, arms folded, peering into the engine through the dissipating smoke like a priestess divining meaning from hazy incense. Could be the carburetor. Or the fuel injector.

Yeah I say. Could be.

Jesus says he knows a good mechanic in the area, but they're not open until tomorrow morning, and do I want a ride home?

I'm tempted to say I'll get an Uber just to spite him but god knows how much the mechanic will cost tomorrow. And, also, probably Jesus would have offered to help anyone, but maybe, maybe, he has been waiting for an opportunity like this to casually get to know *me*.

Despite the nearness of Jesus, the way his car smells like ocean-breezy aftershave that I bet he pats onto his cheeks and behind his ears each morning, the way I can see strands of brown hair slipping, casually, out of his messy-chic manbun, despite all this, small talk is easy. We talk about Ricky's screw up and the big holiday crowds and the Easter bonus. I tell Jesus I'm going to use mine to fix my car. Jesus says he's saving his.

Saving for what?

Jesus glances at me. I haven't told anyone yet so don't like spread it around. But I got into NYU's graduate theater program. He smiles in a way I've never seen him do before. Excited, happy, a little shy. He's younger than me, I realize.

Oh wow that's great I say and because I am also a skilled thespian I make it sound like I am also excited and happy. New York, New York wow.

Then we're outside my apartment. Jesus parks the car.

Thanks so much for helping me out. I unbuckle my seat belt, lean over, put my hand on his thigh. Jesus flushes a little but doesn't say anything so I put my hand to his crotch where his dick is not hard yet but definitely not totally flaccid either.

Hey uh. Jesus peels my hand off his jeans. You're cute but—no thanks.

Well. Okay.

I get out and Jesus drives away, fast enough that he probably doesn't hear me yelling you think you're too good for me? You think you'll find anything better in New York? You won't, you won't, you won't.

At home I change into sweats, pour vodka and low-cal orange juice into the only clean dish I have, a souvenir mug from work, and google NYU graduate theater program. My eyes slide over the application details with no real expectation that I would do the work of putting together an audition tape, resume, statement of purpose, or that another degree would give me anything but more student debt. I finish my drink, close my laptop, and pour another.

Cassie says I need a hobby. I say working out is my hobby and she says no, a real hobby, but what does she know. Today is upper body. I watch my form reflected in the window—stable core, relaxed shoulders, lift and inhale, lower and exhale. Mug Jesus watches me, too. He looks like he thinks I'm wasting my time. Carlos didn't cast me as Jesus when Old Jesus left, he's not going to cast me when New Jesus leaves either. I keep lifting until my arms feel like Jell-O. Then I pour another drink.

I sit down on my mattress and I think, I could masturbate now. I don't want to but the possibility is there, I picture myself pulling my sweats down and reaching into my boxers with sweaty hands and that is enough to start a twinge in my groin so that, as if possessed by a horny spirit, I find myself doing the very thing I don't want to do. I imagine the thorns pressing into Jesus's scalp like fingernails digging into the skin of my back, imagine his outstretched arms embracing me against his hard abs, that single tear running down his cheekbones and into my open mouth salty like precum, I imagine inhaling ocean-breeze aftershave as I suck on his earlobes and pull at the locks of hair that have slipped from the elastic band until he's begging me to jerk him off I think about Jesus all the time while jerking off but never Jason and this feels like a transgression like I just started touching myself on stage and I want to stop and I don't stop until I come on the heathered-gray cotton of my boxers. Then I pull my boxers all the way off, toss them in a corner, and go into the bathroom where I lay naked, face down, on the cold tile, waiting to throw up.

Cassie picks me up for work early the next day. Roman Soldiers 2 and 4 are also early. We sit spread out on the dressing room bench like birds on a telephone wire, drinking coffee or soda, checking our phones. When Carlos comes in, we all stand up.

Heads up Carlos says. He tosses me the spear. The prop is lighter than it looks. You're Longinus.

Thanks I say and I think thanks for your pity. Thanks for this scrap you've deigned to throw my way.

Cassie pats me on the shoulder. Nice going, bud.

I walk out on stage ahead of the Roman Soldiers. The boards feel no different beneath my sandaled feet, the spear in my hand does not invigorate me, but I'm a professional so I haul myself up straight, thrust my chest out, and play the part I've been given.

Jason closes his eyes. The gong reverberates out of the speakers. I lift my spear and stab it into the blood packet taped just below his ribs—too hard, he winces for real. Ripper FX Slow Flow splatters across his ribcage and flows down his side, onto his loincloth, down his cum gutters.

The crowd boos. I bare my teeth and snarl like I'm the baddest motherfucker in Judea but it's just acting I want to tell them, it means nothing, nothing. Then, when everyone is quiet, Jason lifts his head up. Eloi eloi lama sabachthani he cries. I never bothered to ask Cassie what that means. I imagine Jason is telling me that I will never know how great it is to die every night and come back perfect, triumphant.

Freesia McKee

Donkey Fish

The sun is coming up, but I do not know where the hell we are.

I am in the driver's seat. On the upholstery. She is leaning over me, pressing through me. Into the seat, into her.

After the bar closed, she told me to come here. Drive here. *And here and here.* Her hand between my head and neck.

At the edge of the parking lot, goats and cows and roosters bray and call from the other side of the fence. In case you didn't notice the edge when you drove in before dawn, the fence waves like a flag or extended hand delineating the perimeter. *Ahoy, there's the edge!*

The older I will get, the farther I will run away from my human animal. (Perhaps the prodigal son is internal—one's own wandering human animal.)

So what is the fence for?

The fence is for the *animals* in us as much as the fence is for the *humans*. Such a friendly barnyard, though I've heard the donkeys bite.

**

In Kaleidoscope, like every gay bar I've ever been to, there was stale drunkenness in me and Lukas's co-workers, cigarettes on the patio, inside, the small frames of girlfriends winning at billiards amid the fish tanks' humid glow.

How can we be pulled so many ways at once?

**

She's done with cigarettes, with booze, with all hard drugs.

I wonder who feeds the fish now that swim around the gay bar's tanks, looking for fresh water.

There's a hobby horse at the far end of this parking lot, just two quarters for a bounce.

Or think about how the doorway into that building is a hole in the story of the fence.

Before I closed my eyes, the misty donkey scissored his ears.

I was taught that unlimited curiosity means danger. Safer to stick with what you know. And I was taught about safe sex.

Ride me.

The term "hobby farm" has always felt so pathetic. Like a flippant experiment. Like cruel bi-curiosity. Domestic animals with a predictable outcome. ISO a unicorn. *Make the sound a horsey makes.* Wildness broken, aged out of, kaput.

In the first college poetry class I ever took, I thought everyone was dating each other. Or maybe it was just me, a future GDS (Gender Studies) Major, a would-be LUG (Lesbian Until Graduation).

Eventually, I wanted to prove (to whom?) that I wasn't a LUG, but by definition, I had to wait until after graduation.

I tore all the brass fixtures out of my farmhouse. I scrapped my car and shook it out, searching for lost quarters.

**

These days, I am a LAG (*After*), and a LUG/LAG, linguistic gulag of queerness. I am caught in a loop of proof upon proof. Like you, in math, I was taught, *always show your work.*

In those days, I was a NYAL (Not Yet A Lesbian). I was a WOMAN (Woman Observing Men Accomplishing Nonsense). I was an observant woman, practicing every day.

I repeated the rumor of the student who fucked the teacher (not ours) methodically, a slow heart or source of heat.

Flake. Flake. Flake.

**

In the parking lot or anywhere, she is not my teacher. Except in the sense that each person we encounter is a teacher.

She unhooks my bra and slides the fabric up my sternum.

"You have such a great body."

The donkey's dusty ears flicker.

And then on to what she'll call my "trauma boobs." Nothing new happens when she touches me and I stare into space. She stops when she sees me.

Get tanked. Shit-housed. Fucked up. Get lost. Lit. Terrified.

No matter what, you're always going to be a heartbreaker. He's going to go through life knowing that you were the best thing that ever happened to him. And that he lost you.

This upholstery is unfamiliar. But it covers the vehicle of our story.

And I am. Dirty white soles of my sneakers. Trauma boobs. My personal, certain loneliness. Loose clothes.

**

So, teaching lies in the encounter.

The encounter: teaching lies therein.

I wouldn't want to get caught without an answer to the question, "When did you come out?"

Her hands are like the tails on a kite. She is a kite, a hawk, a holy fuck.

He is excised, weighted and dumped, and for a few years, every time I cross anything that feels like a milestone, I will take pure solace in how far away I drove. Those mornings, I will fill my hobby trough with spite.

**

One of the difficult things about writing is that the learning lies not in the experience, but the reflection.

1) First: Experience. 2) Then: Reflection/Learning/Understanding. 3) Finally: Writing.

But as far as I know, this whole process happens out of order, anyway. *Write* towards understanding through the kaleidoscope of *experience*.

An Amy of One. And Annie of Uno. Am Amble Uf On. Or Army Upon.

Or perhaps it's what distinguishes narrative from lyric.

Use writing as a tool. You'll feel less alone.

Let me reflect because I am the same self as the WOMAN in the car was.

What you're doing is way too complicated.

Allow me! To carry us in this trauma car, my little fence-y, booky-self.

**

I've heard that the donkeys here tend to bite.

To protect the bacterial integrity of my elderly grandmother, my aunt yelled, cavalierly, "No more petting zoos!"

A petting zoo is a kind of hobby farm. A profitable one.

I was a LUGnut, a piece of LUGgage, a LUGie. I was a loggerhead, a LUSY (Lesbian Until Senior Year), la LUCE (Lesbian Until Change Expected). I was a luce woman, an energy source, a donkey fish.

My lower lip swollen like a fighter, I was ready to lunge, to lunch, to light my ladyparts like a paperbag lantern, liable to make landfall in the yard of any landed gentry.

Can't I graduate already to prove I'm not a LUG?

It was yet another attempt to escape the inescapable. The gaze penetrating straight into the tank.

I don't mean to shame straight male desire. I just don't want to be poked. *Caution! Do not approach wildlife. Many visitors have been gored by buffalo. Please do not feed the coyotes.*

Do not:
-Approach
-Feed
-Harass

The lesbian wilds are not a family vacation or petting zoo.

No matter how much you show your work, somebody eventually accuses you of swindle, of leaving something out. Even if you have the right answer.

I would just like to know what a life would be like without constant potential violence. And is my queerness an attempt to escape men who would harm me, the guys who claim their uncontrollable desires are weaponized at nine inches long?

O, a standard piece of ledger paper is a larger dagger. And look at how we've been able to control what we put on that.

**

Glass, glass, glass. You're a piece of glass. You're a girl, a lass, a sassy, glassy-eyed, disassociated classmate. You're the glass fence in the gay bar separating the drinkers from the fish.

You're a loosie bummed in a smoking tent. You're a lit spliff passed around. You're the trash kept in the garage so the opossums don't make a mess. You're drug refuse, a spittoon, a self-loathing tiny plastic spoon. The emptiness of the ice cream pint. Bottles half-full of some man's piss floating in the lake.

You're kissing another woman in a car full of trash. Yellow McDonald's wrappers, silvery blue Rice Krispies Treats, crap in the trunk, shiny junk mail, flimsy greasy cardstock boxes from Taco Bell. Once food. Soup-stained uniform piled in the backseat like a nest. Thick black anti-skid shoes.

**

We're parked within the perimeter, inside or outside of the fence.

There's no telling how many of us donkey fish are there.

We are fish who eat other fish, each of us a cannibal, a WOMAN-consuming WOMAN.

We fantasize about getting revenge for our friends at the gay bar, tanked ones we can't liberate, fishy friends we cannot save from the straight men acclimating too quickly to acronymical cynicism. We are penned there, unclear which side of the fence we're tagging.

We are maturing as female *ANIMORPHS*. The unicorn catchers are out there, attempting to poach their would-be's.

Like *Jumanji's* Van Pelt.

I should pause here to say that I'm not shaming the unicorn or the would-be unicorn. But I would like to call out the poacher.

Somewhere, there's a straight man who sees the gay bar as an assembly line and himself as a grandiose Mr. Ford. The straight man who sees the gay bar as his system. The philanthropist puppeteer straight man's subject position: his watery, watery harem. He admires the water feature. He loves a leggy, unicorn-y LUG.

We are the petting zoo in the earliest minutes of morning, before human keepers arrive, and we are aware of ourselves as animals.

I am drawn to her as much as I am afraid. But it must become a permanent pairing, I think, or we will be a hobby farm. I don't know where else queer animals go.

My head unsticks from the grey upholstery, short hairs left behind. Her hands are swallowtail kites. To be "used up" shouldn't mean you stop feeling a thing. My static energy, the burnt end of the roach. When she stops, I step out of the car, but the human in me walks right back. I learn the day's animal lesson.

**

I am afraid of this story. We are not endangered creatures.

We are growing light like flooded dogwood.

Eight adults on the arc. Sixteen names for Noah's wife: Emzara, Haykel, Barthenos, Haikal, T'ajar, Nemzar, Noyemzar, Noyanzar, Set, Naamah, Amzurah, Percoba, Dalila, Nuraita, Norea, Vesta. Nobody knows who she really was.

Two women in the car.

Diamoric

The body before the body's want
What I yearned for, not a quick lay but a good lie about being
Every day I ask myself if today I will go back
Yes, the always is here, where you placed your bag
(Midwesterners call it "sack," but we can forgive this)
Transformation comes when the god pursues
What do I have to do to get Apollo to notice me?
(With every memory of death a new god is born)
I tried to define myself by who I wanted
       rather than want the self I was trying to define
How I rejected a brighter wardrobe for this drab middle-area
(Every day the way back is a succorless nectar)
Somewhere in Alaska, a blue-gray glacier bear
       just experienced for the first time her own reflection
(Quiet wonder, to be marked an entirely different sub-species by your pelage)
This line about landmarks has been in my head for weeks
I can't remember who first spoke it into existence, my euphoric ungendering
As the rhinoceros charges into the brown watering hole, horn lowered
       to rake the earth, so I dig in my heels
Yes, today I am pink dye & knitted yarn
I am every memory of death I have planted in the silver groves
Where the gods come to lie down on the grass, that is where want comes from
Tomorrow I am whatever survives today
Walking out my door a vestigial reference to all the uncles we could have had
       but lost—taken from us—by Apollo's arrows plague-blistered & shorn
(Late in the night, beside myself with reverence, I take in my mouth a lie:
The body's want, put before the body's need to be rebuilt, will sustain the body
I have not wanted well since the first drops of honey were sucked from my roots)
Somewhere in Arkansas, a blue-winged Diana fritillary butterfly on a goldenrod
       will change the world with a sneeze
How I detected a landscape by the shape of its absence
Where are the skyscrapers, eternal horizon of the edgeless plain?
How I detected euphoria by the absence of gender
Something is taking shape in the middle of the black-blue pond
(Keep the names of the muses, o mighty water, I am looking for my own)

It was passing through, it was going apart: the laurels, the purple crepe myrtle
A Dionysian party ends only for the Bacchanalian orgy to begin
If I could keep going like this for days all my grief might be sated
       by some boy uptown
How did I not know this name for what all along I could have been?
(Not one thing but many, not many apart but finally a single self)
A diadem, jeweled aloneness, crowns my head like a honeybee
Yes yes, lyricless song, for you I will surrender
For you will I forsake my want for wings

American Ode: Gender

O   omnisexed self-pollinating angiospermae
flowering plants, magnoliophyta

seeded am I with misgendered remembering
seeded was I by your promise of bloom

O   when they say gender euphoria
they mean a group of teens hyping you up
in a Target when you tell them your pronouns

O   pronouns, I admit I have not fully forgiven you
for failing to encompass the fullness of my being
in a single referential utterance

disassembled matryoshka doll, disbanded band of thieves
sniffing around the rectory for a glimpse of holy silver
& what are we left to call them by if not each name-by-name?

O   variegated vicious alligator smile my father captured
yesterday by the lake in Florida he stumbled upon
while looking for a good bagel

whipped out his camera right there & shot that gator
short of losing his arm to her teeth

here's the gator, closer than it looks
he texted when he sent me the picture
& then, below:
Ur my No 1!!

O   genderless, o gray-eyed maiden goddess who stole my pronouns
maybe I do want to be someone's number one
& I know I swore I'd stop doing this; but, yes, I'd like to begin
with my father

O   gainless approval
          or
awkward gangliness of limbs, how to celebrate something
too small to call victory, too big to call just another text

this text I create as I sublimate poet & poem into one
for every densely woven olden wyrd, a justly chosen broken word
sits in my chest unstitched a hoard of ghostling verbs
jump & rope & gun & pill & knife & tub & blood & blood & blood

O   to be free of the body but not have to cut the body away

O   to be the marble the sculptor shaves off, not the shape beneath he seeks
but the shards littering the floor unmoored & formless

I tell my friend
we destroy our gender in every poem
& I don't think I believe that but I can't help myself

I do go wanting better ways to be;
I do go wanting into the night

again I think of the stricture not to write of bodies
another trans poet placed on other trans poets—
what else but my body would I write of
when poems begin in the body?

O   for a day I am visible to the invisible remnants revolution discards

relevant remnant
          or
relative revenant

O   hypeless, o shadow of an unnamed antithesis
give me the euphoric body I've been so long denied
& I will make myself the light you need so desperately to see

[SARAH] CAVAR

Tulip Monologue

Yes, we are bodies here, but have you considered the tulips? Their thin waftiness, their crimson points dead-center. Their hiding, their little-bird shrug in the face of the sky and the sun. We are bodies just for now, just within this one date, which is in fact a series (a festival, even) of dates, whose names I remember as I remember yours, that is, in absence.

There is this thing called Amsterdam and when I arrived there were no people in it. We were all passengers, but when I disembarked I saw of nothing in myself. I wished to change it. I wanted to be wanted there by strangers. Anyone I didn't yet know how to haunt. There are apps for this. There are freezing nightrooms popping peach-mango gum out the way of the old gas stove, and there are moments of toe-curling   cold

So (in the usual places) I looked for the queers-like-me the way I looked for, what, salamanders? Worms? Stuff that hides from virgin eyes; after your first, find the ripped-up remnants everywhere like horsehairs. *I don't know how long it's going to take to grow back*, I told her. *I don't remember what it feels like to grow my hair anymore.* And I gave her a story with all the bad parts removed, because she was a vegetarian and embroidery-hooper and said things like *struggling with mental health* and surely she is *too good yet* to hear about all I've cut from myself.

I remember when I cut my hair. It was liberating. That's all. There might be more evading the English. We followed the trail of red and pink and spring and came upon a crowd of tourists all following the same yellow flag several shades darker than the flowers, led by a squat little man whose nipples pierced his t-shirt.

Are you hungry? I know a place with the—with a great view. Of the tulips, I mean. I imagined asking her, Dutchlike, *how are you?* Asking if she ever felt alone here, amid the flowers. I imagined she will answer, Dutchlike, in honesty, and then return me the question like a struck little match, daring an answer before we both go out.

Afterward…my apartment is not so far. If you wanted. If I wanted? I sored at the sight of his tight-bound nipples. Touched my own young scabs. The tulips hurt. I noticed they were damp in the places untouched by sunlight, damp and quiet and invisible.

Yeah, I bet. My thoughts are made of things that aren't   *yeah,   okay*

There are scripts for this, but I only study flowers.

CANTRICE JANELLE PENN

grammar lesson

1. Let's diagram the following sentence:

    My ancestors are not an afterthought.

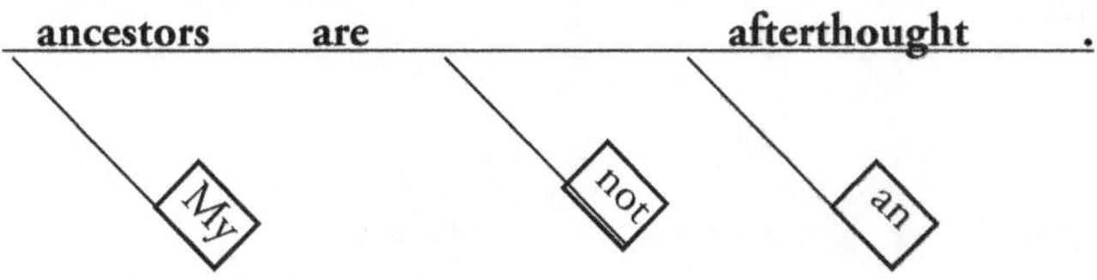

    note the way **afterthought** does not drop off at the end

    & the default to its positive state

    but!

    this is Standard American English & you have to follow the rules

    & yet

    > the letters still feel gritty to the touch, much

    > like the soil that does not belong to us.

2. Define the following root words: **black / black / black.**

    (don't be fooled—these words are not the same!)

    a.) **black:** _______________________________________

    b.) **black:** _______________________________________

    c.) **black:** _______________________________________

there may be at least one more definition of black

but there may not be enough space left on this worksheet

so it will be debated in class.

Grammar Tip: *Enhancing your grammar skills is much easier when you take breaks. So go outside! The air quality is great now, especially with this whole corona thing.*

But don't forget to mask up.

And don't forget that you & your people were never meant to breathe.

3.   As you explore the outdoors, draw a wild bird

in the box below, but!

in its natural habitat

such as an ovenbird, orchard oriole, or olive-sided flycatcher:

what does it sound like?

a.) a quiet observer?

b.) or the exaggerated calls of distress?

Grammar Tip: *Make sure to keep your red pen handy, especially when you're questioned, not believed, stopped and/or searched & questioned again.*

4.   In the following sentence, name the possessive pronoun:

Pyrotechnics at the gender-reveal party set thousands of acres on fire.

5.   Identify any and all gerunds in the following sentence:

Blackfolk are arriving, striving, driving, surviving, living, reliving, thriving, diving, archiving, high-fiving, sky-diving, giving, giving, giving & forgiving.

what do these words have in common? ____________________________

how do they differ? ____

which words have been around for over 400 years, but do not belong?

____

6.   Now, review your worksheet.

Identify the direct object.

This Is My Voice on T

I'm watching *Taxi Driver* and getting absolutely reamed by a stranger in his ugly apartment. *Taxi Driver* is the kind of movie my boyfriend would've wanted to watch with me; the kind of movie he'd have already seen. My ex boyfriend. The only boy I let fuck me while I was still a girl. My name was Daisy. Can you believe that? Crazy. Daisy. I was a stupendous girl. I was a fucking great dyke.

I had an eccentric fashion taste and a short blonde haircut that didn't look at all boyish on my petite head. I wore bras and bralettes. One summer, I found a live baby bird on the sidewalk and I carried it around in my A cup and fed it every 20 minutes with an eyedropper I kept in the front pocket of my boyfriend's shirt. We were always together back then. We named him Bird. He lived happily in my apartment until one day he flew through the door behind me and I slammed it and crushed him dead. I didn't realize until the next morning when I unlocked my front door and found him on the other side; a splatter and a puff of feathers. He was so delicate. My boyfriend cried.

He cried all the time; he was so sensitive. Just the night before, we'd gone from his apartment to one of his friends' and danced separately and together to music pumping from a wireless speaker poorly amplified in a mixing bowl. I was really drunk and so was he; I loved him best that way. I danced my little ass back into him and twisted to whisper in his ear,

"I love you." He jumped away from me, like a game. He was short, but I was shorter and I grabbed him around the waist and pressed my nose into the hard corner of his jaw. "Baby," I said, "I love you," and he recoiled again and said something I didn't hear so I led him to the bedroom that belonged to the friend of his I knew best and closed the door.

I'd smoked weed in there once. The bed was unmade and freckled with ash from the salsa jar overflowing with it on the windowsill. We sat on the cold, exposed top sheet and stared at the alphabetized bookshelf. Boys are so sloppy and alternately so fastidious in these precise ways; I love it.

My boyfriend did laundry more than once a week and changed his sheets constantly. His bed was in the corner so spreading a fitted sheet required him to squat on the bed and push the scrunched hem forward and down over the mattress corner while jumping up to allow the fabric to stretch beneath him. The ceiling was low, so he'd hit his head and I would laugh. In bed, we folded a lot of laundry. We called his bed: Bed Island.

We called it Bed Island because my friend Ian was in love with his friend Ben and once after Ian stood me up I said, "Ian is stranded on Ben Island" and it sounded like I'd said "Bed Island" and we both thought that was pretty clever. On Bed Island, we folded laundry and told jokes and roughed each other up. We fished behind the headboard for loose cigarettes to smoke out the cracked window, or we napped. Or one of us did the crossword in his roommate's

Sunday Edition while the other one napped.

I hate to nap, but I loved to find him sleeping midday with his glasses and his belt and his pack of cigarettes and his lighter and his shoes and his phone dropped like bread crumbs across his bedroom floor. It made me feel like a boy to sleep on clean sheets in a cluttered room. We spent a lot of time in that bed together, not even fucking. On Saturday mornings, we slept in so late we barely had time to eat slices of cold pizza before it was time to go see our friends, or his friends, or mine.

"Baby," I said again, "what is it?" both of us sinking further into the mattress the longer we slumped into it, into each other.

"You only say you love me when you're drunk," he mumbled, not looking at me, "or when we're alone."

When we first began to fuck, all he wanted to do was fist me. Maybe just to prove he knew how? Like a girl scout salute: his thumb crossed tight across his palm, touching just between his boney middle and ring fingers. He also liked to watch me fuck myself with my ex's purple dick. He'd asked me if I wished I had "a real one" and I said no.

Before him, I was a gold star. I know that's a fucked up thing to say, but it was true. And plus, I'm trans now so I can say it. I broke into a persistent cold sweat the first time we held hands in public. I always thought being gay was harder than being straight because it was better. Suddenly, it just seemed harder.

The first time he fucked me in the ass, he was drunk and it was an accident. I was bent over the red couch, the broken one with the innards puffing out. Dick skin surprised me by feeling a little bit like the skin in the crook of your elbow; I just wasn't used to it yet. Later, when I told him what he'd done, he was shocked and apologized but he almost never fucked me any other way.

The next night, we arrived separately to a party where I talked to anyone but him. I went out for a cigarette even though all the other dykes were smoking inside and he followed me out to the street, yelling, "You can't have my dick in your ass one night and then ignore me the next!" Then we started dating.

After that, I never had trouble telling him I loved him. I did it first and more often and with so much honesty, like how I'd just said it at that party. I loved to run into him on the street and yell, "I love you!" I had never done anything like that before. There was a mug of stale water on the bedside table and I drank from it before I asked,

"Do you really think that's true?"

He started to cry. He cried all the time. I wrapped myself around him and we lay for a long time on the grimy bed, me spooning him and him saying over and over again,

"No" and "I'm sorry."

He loved to invite me over and undress me and steer me into the shower and wash me very thoroughly. I would just stare down while he soaped up the tits that hung below my collarbone. He said I had "Grand Theft Auto whore boobs." They'd grown in late so they'd stayed perky, like goiters.

He'd clean my cunt with the long side of his hand between my legs and tilt my head back under the water. I didn't do much but grip him wetly.

After that, he'd rub me all over with a clean towel and after that, if I was lucky, we'd fuck. He'd throw me down onto the bed with a force that was mostly a concession to me and what he knew I liked and drag me by my wet ankles back towards himself and flatten me against the bed with all the light weight of his body. He'd finger me, then fuck me. "It will hurt to come again," I'd say, which meant I was almost on the verge of coming for the first time and he'd flip me over and slip his warm and almost hard enough cock into me and we'd lie like that, belly to belly, for a long time while he'd tell me how much he loved me.

I could hear the music through the thin walls and I wondered if his friends could hear us too, but no one said anything to me when I went to the kitchen to refill the mug with warm tap water. When I returned, he was calm. He hadn't been taking his Zoloft, he said.

Back at his apartment, we showered and had a conciliatory fuck and then a long, deep sleep. He rested a heavy, bony hand on my face all night and I felt very nice and safe.

The next day, when we found Bird, he cried again, and I felt so guilty for killing Bird and for making my boyfriend cry twice in 24 hours. We gathered what was left of him and buried it in the window box because I didn't have a backyard. The window box had nothing inside but cold, wet soil with a thin crust of ice on top. And Bird, I guess.

For the funeral, I wore a peach colored dress that matched my hangover. My boyfriend wore a pair of suit pants he'd bought for the wedding of his ex's cousin. She dumped him before they could attend, but he liked the pants and wore them almost every day with band t-shirts and sneakers that made his feet look very long. He borrowed a silk blouse that could've been a man's shirt except that the buttons were pearlescent and on the wrong side and we smoked cigarettes at the kitchen table and had a daytime gin and orange juice because it was a special occasion and cried some more.

Now that I've quit smoking, I think I might actually be a good influence. Like, on kids or other trans people or my ex-boyfriend; he's a substitute teacher now and still smokes. The clinic made me quit before they'd prescribe me testosterone, which felt a little illegal but not entirely immoral; cigarettes are bad.

I wonder what my boyfriend would think if he knew. Last time I saw him, I didn't tell him. About quitting, I mean. I bought a pack and matched him cigarette for cigarette just like I used to and got so dizzy I ran into a narrow bar bathroom and thought about throwing up, but didn't.

When I started testosterone, I didn't tell him either. He'd come over to catch up and chain smoke on my porch. He was falling in love with the beautiful and accomplished daughter of a very prominent artist. Her work was famous and severe and I couldn't imagine her liking him very much but I could picture him trying to charm her anyway. I could picture him treating her daughter really well, too.

I invited him inside and he hesitated before lighting a new cigarette and bringing it along. He always got a kick out of smoking and sex together. The quilt on my bed is made out of old ties, so it is very silky and masculine. Masculine for a quilt, I mean. He sat down on it and I stood in front of him and took off my parka and then my t-shirt and my binder all at once. My tits were all shrunken but he didn't say anything except,

"I'm just enjoying this." He pointed at me and said, "seeing your body again… " and I thought maybe he could sense or see a change. "There's so much to notice," he sighed, reaching out to touch my necklace, a tiny pink butterfly on a thin pink chain that stained my neck green for weeks.

I sucked his dick until he came sweet and grainy like throwing up in my own mouth.

Afterward, I told him I was transitioning. I only told him because I hoped he might be wondering anyway. He wasn't. My clit looked crazy and I had begun to grow little blonde hairs all over my belly and my tits, like I used to have when I was an anorexic but otherwise I looked the same as when he loved me. "Do you have like, a plan?" he asked. "No" I lied. I'd had the exact same conversation with my mom earlier that month. He told me he was happy for me, pulled up his suit pants, put on his long sneakers, and left.

I didn't see him again for six months and when I did he said,

"Oh! Your voice!" And asked me why I hadn't told him sooner about being trans. I said,

"Because I knew you'd never want to fuck me ever again if you knew," and he pointed to a corner store and said,

"I'm out of cigarettes," and disappeared inside and I thought about just walking away; just disappearing. He reappeared slapping one fresh pack awake and sliding the second into his shirt pocket. He blew through them too quickly to be bothered to flip a lucky, like I liked to do. We didn't talk anymore about it and a few months later I got my tits sliced off and I didn't tell him about that, either.

I thought about him when I first woke up, though. When I sat on the edge of the bathtub and my best friend ran a warm, wet washcloth over my shoulders and under my stinging armpits I thought of him.

People always want to hear the partner's account of a transition, or the parents', or the random bystander's or the ex's. I wonder what he would say about mine. That I look good, probably; happier. Not so skinny.

I remember all these details about him; all these little things that have stayed the same, like his fucking pants. I wonder if he remembers shit about me, or if the things he does remember are still true. Everyone calls me by my new name now but when I pick up the phone he always says, "Hi Daisy!"

"I want to *build* something this summer," he tells me and I don't ask what; probably something conceptual. He won't finish it, whatever it is. He's a very anxious person. Now, I can look at him without absorbing a drop of it.

I'm not a lesbian anymore and I no longer love my ex-boyfriend; he is engaged to the artist's daughter. I have trouble imagining who will love me now; what kind of person. When *Taxi Driver* and the sex ends, I take a shower in this stranger's bathroom and look at my soapy belly.

The stranger's bed is next to the window so I wake up at first light. The night before, I'd watched a teenager back a truck up into the thin space between two weatherboard houses across the street. With the side mirrors pulled in, the truck fit flush; not enough room even to crack the door. I don't know how the driver got out but there he was again the next morning, pulling into the slow cream of dawn traffic. The sex was just okay.

When I moved out of my old apartment and into my new one, I dumped the window box out onto the kitchen table and sorted through the soil until I found Bird's bones. They were bendable, like wet toothpicks, but thinner, like strands of white hair. I cried a little, which I do less now that I'm a boy. Testosterone makes me cry less and admitting that makes me feel like a bad feminist, like an essentialist. I put the bones in an Altoids tin and packed it away. I loved Bird so much, even when he shit all over my books and my groceries. Whenever I left a pot to soak, he'd play in the grimy water and then perch on the kitchen faucet, preening. Of course, you can't live with a sparrow in your apartment forever, but it was so lovely while it lasted.

GWENDOLYN WALLACE

On Flesh

Alone in my bed, I freedom-dream of grasping mango skin between my teeth to reveal a window of golden flesh. My first bite is the most careful. After that, all bets are off. A mango was not meant to be eaten elegantly. I close my eyes and take the plunge, selfishly gathering the fruit in my mouth. As I make my way around the pit, I pick up speed. Drops of unrestrained juice turn the air around me into a citrus cloud. My fingers move by instinct, maneuvering so as to avoid my teeth and also to keep a firm grip on the fruit, which is growing wetter and wetter by the minute. Pulp clings to my face, but wiping it away would throw off my rhythm.

It has been so long since I gave all my senses to this place where hunger and desire meet.

"What do you want me to do to you?" my partner asks, the soft animal of her body pressed against the soft animal of mine. While she awaits my answer, I feel the hunger in her eyes, her mouth, her hands.

I cannot say with certainty that I've ever been attracted to anyone. I want to tell her this as she paints my stomach with tender kisses. I press my nails into the skin between her shoulder blades and she moans into the valley of my clavicle. I want to tell her that when I look at her body, I feel love stir inside me but not a craving. When she touches me, I cannot say it feels more than fine. I want to tell her there is no one I have ever loved more deeply or more wholly. I want her to stay up with me. I want her to cup me in her hands and help me peel apart the layers of love and sex and pleasure and freedom, to show me where one starts and the other ends.

She finishes and removes the condom. I want to ask her to describe the colors of the feelings that consume her when she sinks into my hips, but she turns around and she is grinning. Minutes after kissing me on the forehead she is asleep. Alone, I think of all the ways I want her, and all the ways I can't.

By this point, the mango is so slippery that I am in danger of losing it. Juice now paints rivers down my arms and chin. I stand in the middle of a circle of peels that I have wastefully spat out around me. On the summer day I'm imagining, I cannot tell the difference between sweat and juice and I don't think I want to. Strands of mango kiss the nerves of my fingertips. I fight the urge to grab a paper towel. There are only a few bites left. It's hard work. But oh, is it sweet.

My partner tells me a dream she had about an orgy, glowing as she describes the infinite joy of being immersed in a honeyed sea of words and bodies.

On the nights I slept apart from her, I tried to imagine what red-hot desire coursing through me might feel like. At parties, I jealously watched other Black people explode happily from sweaty crowds in a blur of color, mouths gulping air like fish on a dock. I pictured myself naked in a knot of bodies, consuming on one side and being consumed on the other, and tried to feel aroused by it. The natural stress relief of masturbation became a daily punishment for a body which had isolated me from the salvation that others around me had created in each other. One afternoon, I remember seeing a Black couple passionately making out on a bench. I wondered if their public eros banished the crushing feelings of their precarious existence, if only for a second. I know how few opportunities there are to feel unconfined in this skin.

As I became endless with want, the question of *Do I feel desire?* ripened into the more bitter *Am I less free?*

I drag my teeth against the hairy pit, coaxing the most stubborn hinges of flesh into my mouth. The last drops of mango juice bubble free, stopping briefly in the hollows between my fingers before running down my palm. I swiftly sheathe my teeth and bring the base of my wrist to my mouth, pulling my tongue across my lifeline. Waste not, want not.

It is nighttime and my love and I are laying in the grass together. We do not touch, but I am close enough to hear her gentle breathing. The last full moon of the year that would be greeted by warm weather calls me into her light. I think of everything I love until all the stories become one: the laugh of my best friend, the romance of stem against skin, the warmth of my blood, the loving touch of the women who came before me whose names I do not know. I rub dirt between my hands until it is my palms and dream of the medicines I will make bloom in the spring. I feel my tightly twisted hair grow into the ground like roots. Wanting to give myself up to the beauty of the Earth entirely, I try to spoon the grass.

In a single exhale, I whisper to my partner, "Why would I ever want to be touched by a person when I could be held like this by this earth?" She leaned into the curve of my shoulder, sweaty and free and sweet against my skin. And she laughed. My love, you laughed and all the light left the moon.

I throw the pit into the grass, listening for the delicious thud of satisfaction. In this dream, I savor every drop.

You Win Three Weeks with Jesus

Jay had been to Florida just the one time before. It was the first of a series of gifts from his grandmother, and for the fourth time in their lives, the Harolds family packed their t-shirts and tanks and beach towels into suitcases borrowed from family friends and loaded themselves into an airplane. Took pictures of the dawn breaking over the whole world's cracked and thorny crown, tried not to be picky about the way people's seats piled right into their laps when the seats leaned back, and then they had visited that grandmother all the way down at the end of the world in Homestead, where she lived surrounded by birds and birdseed and her handful of friends who she called her besties. Jay had only seen his grandma in pictures before, and she was doing better off in Florida than Jay had known. It surprised even his mother, whose mother she was.

He remembered the gift store where they bought knickknacks and trinkets to remember Florida, and to remember her whenever she was gone. His grandmother said that to him as he stared down the barrel of a faux rifle, considered its faux heft, went on to survey the variety of snowglobes that rained down not in white flakes but in seaweed, in seahorses, in sand. He had barely met her, and already in the gift store, she was trying to say goodbye.

"Buy yourself something," she insisted, with a voice that was bigger than he had thought of his grandmother. When he had tried to imagine her on rare occasions throughout his childhood, he had seen a tiny figure of a woman sunken at the bottom of an old mason jar, like she was preserved in all her shrivel and her tininess. But this grandmother looked pink, gold, firmly holding to the thick reigns of her long and mysterious life. No one could ever get the truth out of her. But they could have snowglobes.

The second gift was even bigger than just a plane ticket, bigger than just a vacation. It was three weeks at a place called Boys Camp in Christ, as his grandmother explained over the phone in the last week of the school year, instructing him to write down the details for his itinerary. It would mean part of the summer in the swamps of South Florida, not far from where she lived. "You win three weeks with Jesus," his grandma said, her voice even but amused.

When Jay hung up the phone, he did not tell his mother the name of the camp, but he emphasized that it was for Christian youth development. She shrugged, said that if he must go he could do it, as long as she wasn't footing the bill. This time he traveled back to Florida alone, and the novelty of everything sang to him briefly as he tested the twisting knobs of the tray tables, the crunch of the spicy cookies he had declined on the last flight. He kept his hoodie up the whole trip. It was easier that way. People wouldn't stare.

When he landed in Miami International Airport, the warm baking of grab-n-go Cuban sandwiches greeting him, she picked him up in the circle pickup drive with her gleaming blue Cadillac, and he felt the stab of thrill to be picked out of this crowd by the otherworldly beauty of her car. When he felt himself sink inches into the seat, he thanked her for this second present.

"I want you to be who god meant you to be, Jay," was all the reply that she said to him, using his chosen name, and he realized he had no idea who god was, and who god meant him to be, or what the grandma was getting at. The sentence itself seemed as if it was a loosened bookshelf, heavy with notions, but leaning with weight and bad nails, leaning far and seconds from toppling over. He felt the instinct not to put out a hand, not to ask her to tell him what she was driving at, to let it fall.

His grandma's house, small and yellow as a lemon, greeted him from the edge of a pond where other houses as small and pale as fruits stood proud around their view of water. Florida, land of water. Land of in-between.

The Boys Camp in Christ turned out to be less of a camp and more of a highly physical challenge in Christ, as the camp leaders were soon to explain to Jay and a dozen or so young men in their first morning briefing. Most of the boys, he found out, were locals, some of whom had volunteered, and the rest had been put to work as their families had so arranged. Youth service for boys who needed to serve, or else their hands would go elsewhere. That was all it was, on an acreage of what appeared to be the pastor's personal property. They said they were clearing the land for a new church building, but what more details Jay didn't care to hear or find out. He could have been asked to spread horse manure and he wouldn't have felt a difference. Boys who knew their way around a chainsaw could goggle up and start taking down the young slash pines that came between them and their vision. Boys who were less useful got shifts hauling chipped wood or splitting the rest. It looked as if they would pray sometimes in the mornings and afternoons and that would be the extent of the religious nature of the camp.

Before they put a mallet in Jay's hand to start splitting, they went around in a circle and did intros, and Jay's stomach threatened its hot contents at his throat when he heard himself say his name aloud, waiting for a reaction. Told them he was a visitor, staying with his grandma. A few youth group leaders all nodded in unison, knowingly, sanctifiedly, like they had not only secret spiritual knowledge but secret knowledge of Jay.

"Welcome, Jay, we appreciate your service," the leaders said, and most of the boys nodded once or twice, and some of them just stared at the dirt, and one of them smiled.

He had no good idea why the grandmother had dropped him off here, as he came to realize as the hours wore on during that first day and more days were to follow, and yet he felt almost shy about asking her for clarification during their lunchtime phone calls on a cell connection that cracked and broke and struggled to hold the life in their line, even though he was only, supposedly, seven miles away from the grandmother's home. He realized that he now suffered, had agreed and signed up to suffer, in the sweat and heat of this wild swamp place whose strangeness seemed almost incomprehensible.

He was taught how to wield the splitting maul by one of the youth leaders, a wide mustached man with a good looking chin and cheek stubble creeping its way practically up to his eyeballs. Jay felt the joy of being held by the man as he showed Jay how to swing, and for the first time since his grandma dropped him off, he was glad.

"Here's you," said the man, helping him hold his grip on the maul, "and there's your goal." The man pointed with a nod of his thick-haired head. "It's not that you're trying to actually hit the wood, bud. You're trying to swing the weight up"—the man showed him with a swift heave of his thighs as the blunt blade arched into the air—"and then down. One good curve like that. You're not hacking, remember. You're directing the flow." The man spoke in an actively inflected tone, as if he had traveled to many dimensions of other planets and times, had even walked with Christ himself. Jay had never met anybody like him before, and he ate up long glances of him as he walked from camper to camper across the clearing, showing them how to perfect their work, their swings, their shoveling, their stacking. In time Jay grew jealous when the man, who went by Mel, lingered longer with the other campers than with him.

Every day it went like that. Jay sweat like a pig on the day of his own birth. He couldn't feel his hands by the end of it. They took a break only for lunch and prayer, where they sought a moment's shade and drank cool lemonade in the pastor's house, in his otherwise normal person's living room.

His grandma picked him up in her blue Cadillac at night, and every morning she would bring him back to the Boys Camp. Every morning, Jay surprised to wake to the smell of sap and her trailer's dust. He made a habit out of changing his clothes underneath his sheets, in case his grandma ever showed an inclination to open his bedroom door unannounced. Waking in the swamp house, shuffling into his boxers. His grandma feeding him hard-boiled eggs and biscuits with honey, eating with her silently on the formica table that creaked when you leaned your elbows on it.

"Makes a boy learn some manners, that way," his grandma joked. It was the first time she had said the word *boy*, used it to refer to him.

He took an extra long time splitting the wood the next day. Wanting to feel Mel get closer, to show him how, again and again.

One of the last nights in his three Florida weeks he slept badly, hearing the shriek of crickets foreboding some kind of weather under the slash pines. He got hot and then cold, pulling his grandpa's old clothes off and on. His grandma had given them for him to wear—far too baggy in the waist and belly, but he wore the green and red plaid just the same. He rose and stood in front of the bedroom mirror in the dark as the winds blew above the trailer, seeing himself transformed. He could not wear this in his parent's home. He savored it, the idea of who he could be.

Craving something, he found the refrigerator humming and voices trailing from the side porch. Through the screen window, the warm night air blew their voices towards him: his grandma and a woman he had seen walking through the neighborhood each morning, waving as they drove away. This woman touched his grandmother's arm. She was holding something enormous in the other one, and a shadow fell from it and fell across his grandma's face. A great bird hung on the woman's arm, its wings flapping a warning like it would take flight before settling back again, certain that it would stay.

His grandma bent towards the other woman, cooing at the bird. Cooing at the woman. He was sure that he saw it when his grandma's lips bent forward, kissed the bird woman's cheek.

Jay turned away and went quietly back to his room, unsure if his grandma had seen him. He lay under the covers until it was time to chop wood for god another day.

Every now and again Jay would take a look around at his fellow campers—one who had called himself Beau, one whose name he hadn't heard, most whose names he had already forgotten. Chopping, stacking, cutting, grunting. They had no time to talk, and probably that was the idea.

"Yo *Jay*," one of them said to him at last as he came through the open field where Jay swung and missed at logs. "Get out the *way*," he said, looking smug with himself, but the rhymes didn't go far. A tall youth leader caught the snark, reminded them all to keep their eyes on their own races. The other boy scampered off with a gasoline can in his hand, refilling his chainsaw that lay dead in the grass.

Other times Jay would just stare out at the wild landscape of Florida, and then he would stare at his own hands, and then he would look back again at the scrub and pines. The strangeness of all that he saw those weeks in Florida—its alligators, breaking a river's edge; its heat and then cold; its monstrous storms—somehow made him feel more at home than he'd ever been.

"That's it," his grandma said one day as she woke him before dawn. His body aching from the wood. He had dreamed of Mel, in a field where Jesus hung above them and watched and nodded as they kissed, like Jesus was blessing their sacred union. It was uncomfortable for his grandma to appear above him suddenly, with the dream and with Mel's mouth only seconds behind him, vanished now from the blanks of his closed eyes. "We're playing hooky today," she finished, yanking back the shuddering blinds, where the forest light streamed in.

"No Jesus camp today?" he said.

"No Jesus camp today," she laughed.

She took his hand as they walked into the small town. They had hardly spent any time there, and here it was, only a few days until he would leave again for Ohio. He did not want to think of it, but instead he held onto her hand tighter, as if he was a child, suddenly afraid. He wondered what it must look like to these people, to see an old woman in a long purple skirt holding a teenage boy's hand. Of course, they might look twice, trying to figure out what they had just seen in Jay, if they had determined him right.

"I want to buy you a treat," she said. "Like I didn't get to when you were young," she said. She steered him hard into the ice cream shop, where children lined up for superman, rocky road, something on the sign that advertised bubble gum island.

He let himself do this for her. He let himself be her child. They ate a rocky road and a bubble gum island apiece, swapping halfway through, just to show that they were family. They could eat each other's half-licked ice creams.

That night, he watched her peel potatoes the way she peeled potatoes. He sat on the top of her counter and watched her silently, as he could never sit on top of the kitchen counter in his parent's house. She had a peeler, but she used a knife that she moved beneath the skin of each potato, slow and firm like you pop a zit with steady pressure.

"Aren't you afraid you'll cut your finger," he asked her finally. She was peeling potatoes like it was for an army. A great red plastic bowl was piled with the yellow white cubes, far more than they could eat between the two of them.

"No," she said. "But I'm afraid of things that come along and make life too easy," she said, finishing off the last few brown orbs.

The Boys Camp in Christ said its final prayers of that Friday. Their backs, necks, arms aching. They said prayers every day, sang songs every day, and Jay forgot the words to them all immediately. He didn't come to think he was sent here for Christ, and he didn't think his grandma had sent him for that reason, either.

And yet Jay had taken a liking to him, that figure on the cross that they would pray to in a circle under the sky. He watched Christ's carved and wooden face, and it looked like it defied what Jay had known of him before. His sad face tender, yet strong. His body could have fought before he had been nailed to the cross, and yet he had not fought. He was, as far as Jay knew of the story, both god and human. He was both things at once, had been killed because this was too difficult to understand.

The boys all sang, something that ended in hallelujah. It often ended in hallelujah. The faces of the boys around him looked a host of expressions that ranged from unmoved to absent to bored to just sad. Jay had not made any friends here, nor had he cared to. He had not made enemies, and he had not been stalked, taunted, or hit, and that was all he needed right then. Just the quiet. Just the look of the man on the cross. A man who he did not exactly worship, did not believe in as he was meant to believe, but a man whose face he might come to like.

"You can stay," his grandma had nearly whispered, the hours draining down on his last Sunday in her trailer beside the Florida pond. He picked up the snowglobe she kept beside her overstuffed chair, gave it a few hard shakes. He watched the snow come down, in drifts, on top of the one lone house that stood at its bottom. His mother had given this to her, he knew, when his grandma had left Ohio many years ago. *To remind you of a place you'll never come back to,* his mother had said then, with a dark laugh he had never understood. He gave it a shake again, and he thought he saw, for an instant, the little house inside it disappear.

SPENCER WILLIAMS

tranz

                    the story goes   i saw
my face   once   in the reflection of a screen
and thought wow   my face   is not
        what my face is   i guess
if poetry is anything   it is a horse bleeding out
upon the daisies   it is the blurry dick pic
        of a mare

    i'll be honest
i don't care about ur tranz-amorous
                    i am my most
        valid talking shit about strangers
on ur iphone hotspot   accustomed to grief
        i eat   annie's mac and cheese
straight from the pot   over the clothes of
                my dead friends
                    and participate in every game
of hangman   u know   just tranz shit

            it already takes   a certain kind
of muscle to speak   to be heard
    take ur pick   my pronouns: kettle/bell/s
                        rise/and/grind
                        my /neck /my / back

begrudgingly   i am tranz at a time when
the internet exists   now i am nothing without
fetish   in every trans poem   a horse beheads
the lawn and   bucks to climax
        over yellowing grass

            the joke is that   every tranz girl
                named heather or something
                    antiquated / victorian
                goes to grad school
            to play harp   and get surgery

in tranz economy
 a poem   is the same thing as a penny
    ur cum   a kind of direct deposit   in me
look   in the poem about tranz
        the horse
is obviously a fag   i ride off
              on every page
see me   teeth and monstrous schlong

                              see me

SPENCER WILLIAMS

laramie

miraculously / i grew / am grown / woman /
tranny whore / faggot / it doesn't matter / what geography

makes of the word / an erasure / is only a poem
if a body is unearthed / it matters then / that all

my stories / eat like worms / drown in rain /
repeat in anger / faggot of the flesh / faggot

on the porch / it doesn't matter / where
i once existed / or exist / if it is written

when i was young / my parents
drove us through laramie /

and as a child / i knew not one / smear of history /
least of all / a faggot's / but in the car / dad cut

the sound / of a CD skipping /and then /
just the three of us / me / my mom

and him / all quiet / outside / a blur of town /
a ghost / or a gasp / framed by window /

faggot in the blood / faggot in the field /
i didn't know back then / how the middle of nowhere

is also a place / where people live / and die /
but i've been there / in the now / intimately /

miraculously / i am grown / in perhaps
the only time / i can be / here / just barely

SPENCER WILLIAMS

if ur gonna be transphobic at least be funny

the year is 1995, and i am born into the livestream,
        a particle of man continuously
clicking through breasts
            of all shapes in the banner. click me
              says angelbabyxoxo i'm in ur area etc;
and the typeface sticks to me like a threat
       though i mean the good kind
            because in 2021 all i can think of
                  when asked to flagellate
                     over some violent hypothetical is
              yeah, i'm in ur area
                    when someone clicks on me
          just to tell me i'm trans
    which i am
       which i was even when the word
           was confounding   come get me then
                  come do it
             come on now
i'm in ur area.
        it's actually quite
simple: first i was born, and then
        things got boring.
              when i say i'm "online"
       i mean that everyone i've never met
          wants me to know they're disgusted
     by the possibility of my cock
        like i told them to sit there and imagine it
              my loathing staff   my unbearable
pansy rope wrapped viciously around their necks
                         if it mattered
                     i would say i'm no
                     longer
            interested in the forum's
        vocabulary   that i've
          evolved past the need

                                          for fucking anyways

                                                     having replaced my libido

                            with a lust for conservationism

              that i've retired to the mountains

                         of a national park

                              where you can find me explicitly

       not jerking off the grizzly bear

but stroking its coarse fur   feeding

                       the beast berries and kibble

         from the meat of my open hand

like any predator

        the anglosphere has filthy claws

             rupturing all the spending i did on this flesh,

my wiki of shovel-ready tits.

                                       things i might be compared to

                         on the app if people had more vivid

                imaginations: an insect called

                             the japanese giant hornet

                capable of killing 40 euro honeybees

                   in one minute.   if u know   u know

                                    on page-view

                  my tits are shamefully redacted. i speak

                    and 40 women

                            stay pledging my death post-webcast.

               "hornet honey" is what i call their bumbling noise

                    what i call each drop of childless sperm

         what i call anonymous men who stay perpetually in my beeswax

bitch i'm over it

       the main stage   the podium

the this and that of personhood

           just grab me a coffee coke

                and let me smooth my brain out

things were so much simpler back

              when u didn't know me

                but cried watching boys don't cry

if ur gonna be transphobic

       can u not do it in front of my salad

       can u not do it with those bangs

can u not do it with crumbs in ur beard
can u at least be hot
        can u at least make me feel bad   to know we won't be fucking

at the end of the day
    i'm just a woman   standing in front of the door
  of another woman's dms   begging her to take
                her own hate seriously

                            if u have to ask me
                                how i'm doing this week
                                or next   know that i'm clicking
through an endless stream of cat vids for a piece of action
            another article where i am made   a study in cryptozoology

                    at a certain point   u gotta admire the hustle
            of a ghost   despite everyone's efforts   my voice on the EVP
stays repeating

                fuck u fuck u   fuck u

JOHN MORAN

The Gospel According to Fish

1. *Fish Tale*

Good morning, we are fish. Not all fish, but several oceans' worth. We wish to impart the 100% true Gospel of the fish Jesus Christ kept as his pet, Flavius Snook. We shall impart the miracles Mr. Snook performed and the events Mr. Snook witnessed, including mistreatment of fish, multiplication of fish, heavy-handed fish symbolism, and also Jesus Christ's many secret sadomasochistic homosexual initiation ceremonies, which Flavius Snook witnessed from his bowl.

2. *On the Inefficacy of Fish Oil Supplements*

We must proclaim the truth: Fish oil supplements do not do jack. One study compared 23 Land Fish who drank three fish oil lattes a day for five weeks with a group of 11 Land Fish enrolled in an actuary certification course, and those training for actuarial certification were four times more likely to have visited Iceland in the last nine months.

3. *The Magi Present to Jesus Christ the Gift of Flavius Snook*

"Oh my God, you guys have been generous," Mary said, readjusting her secondhand robes on the itchy hay. "I can't believe you brought my baby cologne. He is a little young for all this cologne."

"We didn't just bring cologne," the Magi in purple robes, Esmeralda, said. "We also brought this fish." Esmeralda presented a gilded fishbowl with fig-leaf-shaped feet. Through the glass, Mary saw a small, spikey-finned sliver of silver flit about.

"How lovely," Mary said. "It wasn't on the registry, but I like it."

Esmeralda shrieked. "This fish is not just lovely!" she said. "This fish is to Regular Fish what your son is to Land Fish."

"You mean the fish is a god?" Mary said.

"A savior," said the other Magi, Frank, in pink robes. "Fitting that the Savior of Land Fish shall own the Savior of Regular Fish."

"They must do everything together," Esmeralda said. "They must do everything together or the Ocean shall be murdered. When your son ascends into heaven, he needs to carry this fish. Your son will be on the right hand side of Yahweh, and Flavius Snook will be on the left side. Otherwise, it is foretold that the Land Fish will murder the ocean."

"He'll probably be dead by then," Mary said. "He's just an itsy fish."

Esmeralda stood up. A hay clump snared her robes. "This fish is the Lord, just as your son is the Lord!" Her purple neckline drooped, revealing four parallel slashes on her neck.

"What's that on your neck?" Mary asked.

Esmeralda dropped her purple robe, revealing an iridescent body of green and purple scales. She flopped out of the manger down to the Sea of Galilee, where she jumped in and disappeared.

"I had no idea," Frank said, excusing himself. "If I did, really I wouldn't have come."

"Dispose of this demon fish," Mary said to Joseph as she handed him the gilded bowl. "It can only be the work of the devil."

But Joseph was greedy, and could not part with the curiosity, envisioning an opportunity to charge weary travelers a small fee to view the oddity. He stashed the bowl in his carpentry workshop, sprinkling fish flakes weekly. Mary and Joseph divorced, Joseph was granted weekend visitations, and little Jesus was permitted to keep the fish in his room at Dad's.

4. *Jesus Drops Flavius Snook into the Wine Barrel, and the Wine Is Turned to Water*

Sarah McCrimmon's birthday party was your typical upper-middle-class Nazarene birthday party: pin the tail on the donkey; fig throwing; an adequate garlic hummus spread, "very adequate," one parent said, "a little garlicky;" and an underemployed, clinically depressed clown. "Not Cain as he's slain," the kids groaned, tired of the clown's only decent impression. Do you think the parents were enduring this without booze? No. They had 10 vats of wine, plus hard stuff. Did the McCrimmons, who had their own vineyard, need a five-year-old to wave his hand and turn water into wine? Most certainly not.

What really happened is Jesus was a bit of a showoff. He liked attention and was good at getting it.

"I want to be famous," he'd told his mother.

"You will be, honey, you will be," she said. "Just tell them what I told you to tell them."

"I don't like that story," Jesus said. "I'll show them my fish. I'll get famous with fish." Jesus was holding Flavius in his hands. "Hi, I'm a fish," said Jesus in his best fish voice. "Have you ever met a fish before? Now you have!" Jesus laughed so hard he rolled on the floor and almost squished Flavius before rising.

"I'm a fish, I swim swim swim," Jesus said as he tossed Flavius between his hands. He missed, and Flavius fell into a vat of wine.

Are you a fish? Have you swum in wine? Not fun. Flavius could not die yet. It was not yet time to save all the fish in the world, sacrificing himself so we could eat each other with impunity. So Flavius performed his first miracle and turned the wine into water. Jesus could easily see Flavius swimming now that the liquid was clear, and scooped him out.

"What happened?" Mary asked, rushing over.

"Water," Jesus said.

"Oh my god," Mary said. "You performed your first miracle! Ladies, check this out."

The moms ran over to the vat of wine, which was now a vat of water.

"I love water," Sarah McCrimmon's mom said. "In the morning, before coffee, everyone should squeeze lemon over eight ounces of water, to rehydrate."

5. *Jesus Walks On Fish*

News spread in Nazareth that Jesus had party tricks. The underemployed, clinically depressed clown, Timothy, did not like encroachment in a tight market. Timothy came up with a new routine: Dolphin Clown. "I'm a clown and a dolphin," he said to everyone he met. At a wedding by Galilee, attendees chanted "Dolphin! Dolphin! Dolphin!" while Timothy swam with his right arm, his left arm raised above the water like a dolphin fin. This was extremely popular.

"I've got to give the people what they want," said Jesus, now six, stewing over his fishbowl. "Here's what I need you to do, Flavius. I'm going to release you in the Sea of Galilee. You're going to command the fish to make stones of fish under the surface of the water, and I can walk across them and it can look like I'm walking on water but really I'm walking on fish. Chill?"

Flavius lapped the bowl agreeably.

At Galilee, Jesus released Flavius, and Flavius gathered the fish to create discreet stone-like platforms just under the surface of the Sea, which Jesus ambled across as if he had no worry in the world, impressing the fisherman on nearby boats, whom had found the Dolphin Clown routine overrated.

6. *The 1994 "Gill Net" Ban in Florida Destroyed the Commercial Fishing Industry and Ended the Widespread Consumption of Mullet, a Source of Protein for Generations of Working People*

"Mullet is poor folks food," says Jonas Porter, commercial fisherman, referring to the bottom-feeding fish, the striped mullet, which is the most abundant wild food resource in the US state of Florida, no longer eaten by Floridians. "That's why I like it; I'm poor. Jesus was a net fisherman. He wasn't a brain surgeon who likes sports fishing. He didn't come down from Atlanta in an SUV to catch his precious red snapper one at a time on a pole. No. Jesus and his cronies used a net to feed the multitude. These folks want to make the ocean something you look at not something you eat from. It'd be okay if they knew what they was talking about. But the stuff these people think up. My God, they pull it from the sky."

7. *Fifty Shades of Jesus*

In his late teens, Jesus of Nazareth discovered the effectiveness of sexual activity as a means of control, persuasion, and personal monetary enrichment.

"Ever have sex on meth?" he asked Timothy, when they were finally alone in Jesus's favorite cave, where Jesus, carrying a candle and his fishbowl, showed Timothy ancient cave paintings depicting winged men engaged in fellatio, which Jesus had forged the previous evening.

"No," said Timothy. "Why do you ask?"

"Just seeing if you're open-minded," Jesus said.

"While we're down here, I've got to ask, dude. Are you trying to put me out of business? There's only room for so much fun in Nazareth."

"No," Jesus said. "I just want to make you feel something you've never felt before. Ever had a prostate massage?"

"Sorry?"

"Ever had someone who knows where the prostate is restrain you, stick their finger up your butt, and massage your prostate until you howl in unalloyed orgasm?"

"No," said Timothy. "I'm just a clown who is sometimes a dolphin."

"I'd like you to be my apostle," Jesus said. "I'd like to be your Master. I hold the secrets of the Kingdom."

Flavius wanted to say, Guys, please, get a different cave, but he couldn't speak. He could only swim the shrouded bowl.

8. *Multiplying Two Fish into Hundreds of Fish Is Painful for Fish*

Timothy, who was feeling a little too relaxed, maybe spent one too many nights in the cave, painted posters which read, "My Master Is Speaking on the Hill – Free Fish." When Nazareth's hungriest summited the hill to find a fishless expanse they were right pissed. "Where's the free fish?" they asked. People pointed to Flavius's bowl and asked, "Can we eat that fish?" Jesus said, "No, that's Flavius, as I am to you, he is to fish." People were like, "I don't get it. I'm hungry." Jesus said, "Here, let me multiply these fish my mom packed me for lunch." He leaned towards the bowl, to make sure Flavius heard. "I'm multiplying the fish now. I can't wait to multiply the fish. Flavius, can you hear me? I am going to take these two fish, and ta-da, turn them into many fish. It's going to happen very soon. I'm about to do it."

Flavius obliged. He turned those two fish into hundreds of fish, something only the Savior of Fish could do. It was painful for those two fish, to have their cells split and regenerated. It was the most painful thing that has ever happened to Regular Fish in Regular Fish history, so unlike the Great Flood, the most pleasurable moment in Regular Fish history. We did it for the Land Fish, and what did the Land Fish do for us? You ground horseshoe crabs into fertilizer and farmed catfish in tanks, speared whales with harpoons and let microplastics rain.

9. *Flavius Snook Foretells the Great Dead Zone*

"One day, there will be a great dead zone," Flavius Snook told the kitschy plastic coral decorating his bowl.

"What is that, O great one?" The plastic coral asked.

"Land Fish will desire corn syrup in their water," Flavius Snook said. "So that they may answer their emails. Nutrient pollution from Great Plains stolen and defiled with corn will drain into the Gulf feeding algae blooms resulting in an hypoxic zone the size of Massachusetts."

"Dude, we are so lost," said the plastic coral. "We literally don't get anything you're saying. We're focused on decorating this bowl."

"The coral, too, shall bleach and die," Flavius Snook foretold, "until insolence sweeps away all fragile things."

10. *The Apostles Reveal They've Known All Along Flavius Snook Is The Miracle Worker*

"Dude," Timothy said.

"What," Jesus said.

"Dude, we know, show's up," Timothy said.

"What show?" Jesus said.

"Take me to the cave and I'll tell," Timothy said.

"You horny slut," Jesus said.

Jesus took Timothy to the cave. They assumed the positions.

"Master, I have a confession," Timothy said.

"Give it to me," Jesus said. "Give me your all."

"We know it's the fish."

"You blaspheme me," Jesus said.

"It's the fish that is divine!"

"You need a spanking!" Jesus said. "A heartfelt hand."

11. *Flavius Foretells the Life of Robin, Who Will Spend July 2010 Removing Oil from Hermit Crab Shells*

"One day, there will be a great saint, Robin," Flavius foretold to the plastic coral. "She shall be an unpaid volunteer at the Gulf Islands National Seashore in Biloxi, Mississippi. She shall be 27 years old, the bearer of three children, one from her first marriage to Doug, she shall teach Civics at Colmer Middle School in Pascagoula. On Tuesday and Thursday afternoons, for three weeks in July of 2010, she shall drive her children half an hour to the Gulf Islands National Seashore Visitors Center, where the Biological Sciences Department of Auburn University will organize marine creature cleaning stations. While the two young children play, she and her oldest daughter Lan will sit on folding chairs tucked into a folding table, using toothbrushes to scrub oil off hermit crabs, those crabs who make their home in shells of snails.

"A decade later, she will lose her husband, Viet, to sea. Robin will fill an empty glass lamp with shells, praying for his soul every time she drops a shell in the lamp, until its hull overflows with cockles and angel wings and lady slippers and sand dollars and olive shells and lightning welks. When she and her children flee Hurricane Oglethorpe, the lamp with its ocean-blue shade will be the only non-essential possession fit in the crowded sedan."

"It's like decorating fish bowls," the plastic coral said. "You've gotta fit ten gallons of shit in a five gallon bucket."

12. *The Fish of Christ*

"Take this fish, all of you, and eat it," Jesus says, as his apostles gather in the cave for their last BDSM-themed supper.

"Oh my God, did you cook Flavius?" asks Timothy. "You're so dramatic."

"This is not Flavius," Jesus says. "This is Flavius's brethren. As I was saying: This fish is my body. It is the new and everlasting covenant. It will be fried for you and for all, so that your sins may be forgiven. When I die, hold fish fries at the volunteer fire department to remember me. When you slather the fried fish in Kraft tartar sauce, you will be slathering me in Kraft tartar sauce."

13. *Logistical Decision*

Under Pope Tangerine IV, the Church switched the Eucharist from fish to bread out of food safety and preservation concerns, despite the urging of seafood industry lobbyists to at least try canned fish.

"Jesus does not come in a can," Pope Tangerine IV said.

"But fish do," the seafood lobbyists said.

14. *Why, in the State of Washington, Is Wheat Moved by River, but Salmon by Truck?*

Locks at dams allow the movement of barges along the Columbia River. These barges carry Washington's wheat. The salmon are retrieved from the river on the near sides of the dams and trucked, in tanks, to the far sides. Why can't you put the wheat in trucks, and the salmon in river? We fish would like to know. This is one of the questions we fish ferry. There are other pertinent questions we hope to relay from our world to yours.

15. *Pontius Pilate Dips his Hands in the Fishbowl*

"Please, I beg you, also crucify Flavius," Jesus asks Pontius Pilate, as the Roman guards strip him, bind him, and humiliate him using the effective BDSM techniques of which Jesus is all too familiar. "He needs to die for fish sins as I die for man's sins, then we can fly to heaven together holding hands. Or, mixing fingers and fins. He is my divine non-human brother."

Pontius Pilate looks down at the little fish in the bowl. To Jesus he says, "You are really a piece of work."

"That's my fish," Jesus says. "The most important fish in the world."

"You are really a big personality," Pontius Pilate says. "Fine, we'll string up your fish." Pontius Pilate makes a move for Flavius. Being divine, he proves difficult to catch.

"You can't even catch a fish with your hands!" Jesus says. "What kind of a Prefect are you? Sad!"

"People are watching!" Pontius Pilate whispers, his hands moving furiously in the bowl. "Cut it."

"I am a fisher of men, but you are not even a fisher of fish!" Jesus says. He cranes his neck around the pole to which he is bound to see if the crowd is getting a load of this.

"I'm not trying to catch a fish in the bowl," Pontius Pilate announces loudly to the crowd. "I'm just washing my hands, cleanings myself of this whole debacle."

After Jesus is given his cross to bear through town, Pilate orders Flavius fed to dogs, but Flavius escapes the kennel, flops himself to the foot of the cross, survives on the salt and water of his keeper's tears, until there are none.

16. *The Oceans Destroyed*

We could explain that 90 percent of native oyster reefs are gone. We could remember how the mullet used to run in late fall, a black wall of fish like a tsunami, bounty along the shores. We could give you Excel sheets of sea urchin distribution. We could ask that you catalogue the colors of coquinas, act surprised when there are none to be found. We could replace every barnacle in the ocean with eyes, and still, would you see it? Could your riches turn back to plankton even if you realized what is worth measuring?

17. *We Value Your Feedback*

Thank you for listening to the Gospel According to Fish. We are happy to answer any further questions, as we know this version of history may be surprising for those to whom key information has been withheld. Please tell your friends and loved ones about our unique perspective on these significant events. We also value your feedback as we work to perfect this tale for its target audience.

It is our truth that Flavius died at the foot of the cross so that our sin of eating each other could be forgiven. We have been here in this eddy, for many minutes now, trying to get these points across to you, and now we have become as friendly as we are hungry. We are very near the moment where we eat each other, another day closer to what is foretold. We chase and flee and eat, we are fish. We were the Body of Christ, before bread. We are the bread that swims.

KENDRA MACK

The Animal

Is cod a vegetable? I wish I could ask someone. The menu says that it's Boston baked and comes with a side of asparagus. Cod must be meat. There are only three entrée options because the company is paying for the meal. This keeps us from going wild, I've learned. I start reading the other two options and am startled to hear my name.

"Eunice!" It's a woman named Tracy, seated to my left. I work with her, but I don't really know her. "You know what, Eunice?" she says. "You remind me so much of me, when I was your age, just starting my career. The skirt, the tights, ah, all of it. I looked just like you!"

She tips her wine glass to mine. I put down the menu and we clink. I swallow and smile. There is nothing I can say. The poor woman means well. She can't know that the possibility of one day becoming her makes my insides buck and snort. That it is impossible. She's too thin, her eyes too wide, teeth too short and straight, her hair a short, straight bob. I could maybe pull a bob off, but I'm not sure that I'd want to.

It's 7:27 Eastern Time, and I might be starving. Plates of ugly oyster appetizers have just landed on the table. Who ordered them? They stink and my co-workers slurp from shells. I can see their tongues. This is all normal, apparently.

How many corporate dinners has Tracy been to in her long life? I should ask her. How many years and how many glasses clinked in a dim-lit restaurant after a nine-hour day of meetings and whiteboarding and team-building activities involving Post-it notes and PowerPoint presentations in a hotel conference room? But I don't want to know. This is my first dinner like this, and I'll keep smiling, not too wide. And I should smile, because if Tracy thinks that I can someday be her, then my disguise must still be working.

Amy taps Tracy on the shoulder, distracts her with a question about where she got her earrings. Finally, I can focus on the menu again. *Tuna steak with*... no steak. No, no steak. *Almond-crusted salmon with roasted broccoli*...I could maybe scrape the almonds off? That might be a tasty treat. And then there's the cod.

"Cod, really? Blech. So bland." I overhear Jackie say to Jaimie, on my right. "Who would ever choose the cod over tuna?" Tuna, the table murmurs. Oh, yes, definitely the tuna. Tuna. Steak. Tuna steak, steak. My nostrils are sweating.

"I'm more of a salmon man myself." This comes from Thomas, seated directly across from me. I look up and am surprised to lock eyes with him. Thomas's eyes are dark brown, framed by round, smart glasses. I should get glasses like that, I think, and a silk neck scarf, too, just like that one, and a floral shirt. Thomas is on my team and yet I haven't noticed how stylish he is until just this moment. It's a miracle how long I've gone without noticing. Four months? Since I started the job. His smile is a thin kind of smirk.

"What about you Eunice? Have you decided?" Decided what? Oh. I don't know. The tuna, maybe. The tuna comes with rice and spinach. I should eat some greens.

A bell dings and I jump, knocking my knee hard against the table. The bell keeps dinging. *Ding ding ding...*right. It's not a bell, I should know this. It's the sound of a knife tapping on glass. The table quiets and Tim, our Senior Director and man-in-charge, stands before the nine of us. He smooths his tie against his firm belly, raises his red wine.

"I'd like to say cheers to a successful day of team-building." Jackie and Jaimie woop woop! together. "I know we're all running hard every day and so I think it's important to take a time-out every now and then to really get to know each other. I think if we can work better as a team, we can improve as a team, and I think…" Thomas is still staring at me. He's not staring. He's looking down at the menu. Now I'm the one staring! I wish he would open his mouth. I want to see his teeth. His eyelashes are so long, they press up against his glasses. Do humans have eyes that are that dark?

"Eunice!" Tim has shouted my name. Oh no, what did I do? All eyes are on me. "Cheers to our newest team member! Up and running so fast, you'd think she's been with us for years. What a valuable addition to the team you are. We're happy to have you."

Happy to be had. My voice is small compared to Tim's. The table laughs. It's a reaction, anyway.

Cheers! I'm going to get it right this time. Cheers! Gently touch the wine glass to everyone else's glasses, even if they're out of reach. Cheers to Thomas! Cheers to Tracy! Reach across the table, crossing other people's arms. Cheers to Jackie, Jaimie! Get tangled up, let people put their stinky armpits in your face for a second. It's important to cheers! This will be the first cheers of many tonight. It's now only 8:05. Only! I hope that no one can hear my stomach roar.

"So Eunice, is your family from around here?" Oh no, they're from the Midwest. "They must be so proud. First big job out of college. You're lucky, especially with the job market the way it is." Oh yes, they're very proud. "She's not lucky, she's talented! We wouldn't have hired her if she wasn't a sure bet. Did you get a look at her portfolio? She's a star! Now what do your parents do for work? Does talent run in the family?"

I'm saved by a waiter appearing over Tim's shoulder. Everyone fixates on their menus. What is everyone ordering, again? The tuna, right. They'll forget the interrogation and that's a good thing. I don't want to lie too much. I couldn't tell them my mother was euthanized two years ago. Shot in the head and burned to dust. I was six. Back at the orchard, my father is still pulling carts at 30, older than any horse should have to work. That's if he's still alive. I could say I ran away, but I didn't. He wanted me to go. He wanted me to go to the east coast, to go to college, to be with the humans, so I wouldn't have to be pulling carts my whole life like he has done. I can have a shot at freedom, or at least a shot at earning it.

And it's not like there's a law that says I can't be here, working for this company, eating dinners on their dime. But there's also no law that says I can, and it's rare. It's best not to stand out, best not to give them a reason to look too long or think too hard about what I am.

I'll have the tuna. Please. The waiter scribbles my order, leaves. Tracy pours me more red wine. I don't want more. It's the color of blood and smells bitter and makes my mouth dry and stains my teeth black. Everyone's teeth are stained black here, though. They don't seem to notice or care, talking and laughing wide open. Everyone except Thomas. I still can't see his teeth. I should try to make him smile.

I see he's already looking at me. "Did you get the salmon?" he asks. No, the tuna. "What?" He can't hear me, or I'm hard to understand. He leans forward. I lean forward, too. I think I see his nostrils flair. No, I got the tuna. He shakes his head, his hair, gelled perfectly still, doesn't move. "Do you like the pinot noir?" The what? "The wine." I look at my glass, the full cup of blood. I must make a face because Thomas laughs. "I feel you. Cheers to that." He lifts his glass, and I mine. His teeth flash white and maybe crooked for exactly one second, not long enough to know for sure.

Our ding sends the table into an uproar. "Cheers? Is this a cheers?" Amy asks, and suddenly everyone is in cheers! When it's over, Thomas and I don't sip.

"My family is from the Midwest, too. I grew up in Ohio, actually," Thomas says. "I thought you had an accent." Missouri. I don't have an accent, neither does he. He changes subjects. "The hotel we're staying at is great, isn't it? The company went all out. We must've had a good quarter, don't you think?" He knows better than to keep talking about our families, about us, who we are and where we're from. I nod. I do think we've had a good quarter. I'm going to ask him where he got his glasses, and his shirt—

"I don't know what it is, horses just love me." It's Jackie. Jaimie beside her slaps the table, cackles. "I know! Remember that time we were at the Topsfield Fair last year, and that horse kept coming up to you in the barn? It followed you around like it loved you! Yeah, that horse was all over you!" Tim is listening to them, as are others. They're nodding, laughing, and now me, and Thomas, too…half the table is now engaged. Jackie shrugs, smacks her lips after a sip of wine. "I don't know what it is."

Jackie is another one I haven't looked at too closely until just now. She's a basic woman, a young one, younger than Tracy, older than the one I'm pretending to be. But of course horses would love her. Who wouldn't? She's petite and sweet, like an adult child almost, like she'd be glad to feed you out her hand while rubbing your forehead, telling you how beautiful you are. Her shirt has tiny white birds patterned all down the front and the sleeves, and her pants—how have I not noticed the pants? They are tan, tight, like riding breeches. For one, maybe two lucid seconds, I'm imagining her riding on my back, as I run, gallop away from this stupid seafood restaurant, full-speed, knocking over tables and spilling wine as her legs hold tight to my sides.

"Eunice." It's Thomas again. He points behind my shoulder, where a waiter stands ready to pass me a plate. The tuna has arrived, and it's far worse than I'd feared. I don't understand what I'm looking at.

This isn't like any steak I've seen before. It's pinkish purple and it's wet—at least most of it is. The edges are grey-beige, covered in black and tan flecks that remind me of flies and worms collecting on dead flesh. All of this sits in a pool of blood. It must be blood. What else could this red water be?

Is this blood? I ask Jackie, against my better judgment. She stifles a laugh, hiccups. "No,

Eunice, it isn't blood." Then what is it? "I don't know. Haven't you ever had tuna before?" Her own plate of tuna is set down in front of her. "It's some kind of vinegar. Probably."

If it's some kind of vinegar, then I might still be able to eat the rice and spinach that sit in the liquid. I can eat from the top, work my way down. Maybe then it won't be obvious.

"Should've gotten the salmon." Thomas places his napkin in his lap. The salmon before him is also an uncomfortable slab, but at least it isn't bleeding, and it's covered in chopped almond pieces. What's more, his has come with a side of soft stubby carrots. I thought the salmon came with broccoli? "It did. I don't like broccoli, so I asked for carrots." To ask for carrots. The idea didn't even cross my mind. "If you want something, just ask for it. You'll learn. Don't worry." I'm not worried. Thomas forks a carrot into his mouth. "You want one?" No thanks. "Are you sure?" Yes, I'm sure.

I'm hungrier now than before, and I think I'm ready to try a small bite of spinach. But now I become aware of the smell. The smell. Worse than the oysters. Worse than anything I've ever smelled and was supposed to eat. It's unnatural, this foul tuna. And yet my co-workers eat, cutting through the purplish flesh, stuffing it in their mouths, chewing, washing it down their throats with wine, and I don't understand. The air is so stiff with fish, I want to cry and stomp. Instead, I put a little spinach in my mouth, chomp one, two, let it slide down. Rice next. Breathe in. Chomp one, two. Let it slide.

I pretend to listen to Tracy and Amy's debate about the quality of the hotel's shampoo samples. They sniff each other's hair. I nod now and then. The tuna under my nose only smells stronger, and I try to remind myself that there are many worse odors. Pig shit. Cow blood. The smoke from the fire on the night my mother's body burned. Still there are some smells I miss, like fresh hay and the orchard in summertime.

"What's the matter, Eunice? Not a fan of the tuna?" It's Tim, the boss.

"She thinks it's sitting in blood," Jackie says. The traitor. I'd buck her off my back so quick she wouldn't know it's coming. Tim chuckles, "So what, a little blood never hurt anybody." I look to Thomas, hoping for some sympathetic gesture, but he's hunched over his plate, busy digging in his food, fast and hard, both wrists bent at awkward right angles as he cuts, forks, shovels up to his mouth. The carrots are already gone. Only a small clump of rice and a nub of fish is left, but not for long. Even if I were to call out his name, Thomas, he probably wouldn't hear me, he's so focused. I watch in awe as he gobbles up the last few bites like one, two, three—

Cheers! It starts at the other end of the table. We all raise our glasses for a reason unknown to me. This, together with his clean plate, seems to snap Thomas out of his food trance. He looks around bewildered. Cheers!

I have to try the tuna now. I fork off a small corner, mostly avoiding the raw red center. Big breath in. I put it in my mouth. I can't even chew it, can't swallow. I'm gagging. I'm choking quietly. I have to spit it out. I can't spit it out. It's dissolving into something on my tongue. I squish it around. My eyes are watering. I can't see.

From across the table, Thomas hands me my glass of water. I grab it and gulp. The tuna goes down with a shiver and shake. Thank you.

"Hey," Thomas says, leaning over his clean, white plate. He's sharing a secret with me and the secret is: "Don't eat it if you don't like it."

I excuse myself to the bathroom. My nostrils are definitely sweating now, everything is, and I have to go deal with it. The bathroom is empty and fancy, tiled black with black shiny toilets. I close myself inside of a stall and take a deep breath. I stand still, imagine that I'm in a stable, my mother in the one beside me. I can almost hear her stomping, knocking on the wall between us, telling me to stick my neck out, she wants to see me. When I do, I show her that I'm still here, nowhere else. This is the only peace I will feel tonight.

The bathroom door opens to giddy laughter and stumbling high-heels. "I'm telling you girl, you gotta get back out there," one woman says to the other. "I knowww," says the other. It's Jackie and Jaimie. I recognize their voices. Jackie enters the stall next to mine, and Jaimie on the other side of her. They start peeing at exactly the same time, and I don't move. "Tim is cute. What about Tim?" "Shut up, he's our boss!" "Well, what about Thomas?" "I don't think I'm his type, if you know what I mean." I don't know what they mean, and they mustn't know I'm in here. They flush at the same time, too.

"Eunice is an odd duck, isn't she?" "Yeah, really. She barely ever talks. But I like her. She's very pretty. I need to ask her about her skin care routine." "Oh yeah, I like her too. I just think there's something off about her, you know? You know, I think she might be—" A whisper.

"Oh my god *stop* it!" The bathroom door slams, and once again I'm alone in sweaty silence. I wrap some toilet paper around my hand, use it to pat dry my neck, my nose, my forehead, behind my ears. I dab around my mouth, which still tastes like something awful. Like dead tuna steak. I flush the paper, stretch my arms up over my head, as high as they will go, until they hurt.

I leave the stall, take a quick look at myself in the mirror. I am very pretty.

Back with my colleagues, I'm relieved to see all tuna has been removed from the table.

"I told them they could take it," Thomas says. "I hope you don't mind." Not at all. He hands me a menu that's being passed around the table. "Ready for dessert?" Dessert. Right. It's 9:24 and my hunger has been overrun by exhaustion. I want to go back to the hotel, but that can't happen yet. Now there is dessert, and we will be here for another hour. Enough glasses of wine have been consumed that the conversation flows and will keep flowing. The humans will be happy and free to talk about whatever they please, silly or serious. They will order coffee with more sweet alcohol in it.

The two dessert options are carrot cake and a brownie sundae. "Who would ever choose carrot cake over a brownie sundae?" I would, Jackie. I love carrot cake. All I want in the world, besides a bed to sleep on, is carrot cake.

"And for you, sir?" "I'll take the cake," Thomas says, glancing at me. "And for you, miss?" Carrot cake, please. "Very good choice."

When the carrot cake arrives, it is a tall and wide cube, two thick layers with luscious golden frosting spread in the middle and on top. Yum. Suddenly famished again, I find the nearest silver spoon and start eating, even before everyone has received their brownie sundaes.

"Don't you want a fork for that?" Jackie asks, but my mouth is too full of cake to answer her. I would eat it with my face if I could. Eat it with my face while she pats my head, right behind the ears. Such a pretty horse. Hungry. She loves her carrots.

The cake is gone already. I sit back. Tim asks, "Was it *that* good?" Yes. Best carrot cake I've ever had! Sweet. Creamy. Carroty. Thomas slides his dessert plate towards me. He's already eaten a corner off the cake, but that's not a problem for me. I pick up my spoon again, not waiting for him to ask. Thank you. "My pleasure. It's all yours."

Once I've had my second dessert, word has gone around the table about how much I love carrot cake. "She ate two whole pieces!" "Wow!" "Good for her! Good for Eunice." "I knew I should've gotten the cake." "Now I know what we can get her for her birthday. Hey Eunice, when's your birthday?" Cheers! Cheers to Eunice and her carrot cake.

People lift their coffee drinks, steaming out of fancy glass mugs. I lift my spoon, licked clean. The table erupts in laughter. I laugh too. A young couple at a nearby table looks over at us, disturbed. They're jealous of all the fun I've just caused.

Then there's a hand in my hair. I don't feel it at first. But then I do. It's a graze, a brush, a slight tug from my left. I jump away from the hand, which I now see is attached to Tracy.

"What shampoo do you use? Don't tell me you used the hotel shampoo." She smiles, black teeth, wine-heavy eyelids. "What shampoo do you use?" she repeats. She's still touching me. Stop. I don't know. Please stop touching me. I lean away, and her smile stiffens.

Another hand, this one firm, lands on my right shoulder. This time I really jump, leap, knock both knees under the table. It quakes and a half-empty wine glass goes over, spills forward into Jackie's lap as she snaps her hand back and cries out: "My paaaants!" Her tight tan breeches are soaked red in pinot noir around the crotch and thighs. "I can't believe this! These were my favorite!" Jaimie sacrifices her napkin to her friend's pants. "Don't rub!" Jackie snarls. "Rubbing will make it worse!" She seizes the napkin, presses it between her legs. She looks like she's about to cry. I want to say sorry.

"Why are you so *jumpy* Eunice? I was just going to ask you about your skincare routine! You don't have to be so *jumpy!*" All my co-workers, Tim, Thomas and the others, they all silently stare at Jackie, at me. They assess my jumpiness. Yes, I am jumpy, pretty, carrot-cake-loving, and I have good hair.

I stand up, unsure why. I have to take this call. That's why. Sorry everyone. Sorry Jackie. I'll buy you some new pants. I push my phone up to my ear and rush toward the exit, weaving between tables and clouds of fishy odors, two legs not quick enough to carry me out.

Crossing the threshold, I'm outdoors, finally, on a city sidewalk. The Boston night air is cold. I should need a jacket, but I don't. I check the time on my phone. It's 10:06. I've been at the restaurant for three hours. It feels like much longer. Across the street is the hotel, its revolving glass doors shine like daylight. A taxi pulls to the curb in front of me, blocking my view. A man and a woman get in. Cars honk at the taxi. It's taking too long. Cars honk everywhere, on every street. Three young boys punch each other's shoulders and laugh as they walk by me and I wonder where they're going.

Thomas is suddenly beside me, one hand fishing inside the pocket of his stylish brown coat. I say hey. "Hey is for horses." Better for cows. "Pigs would eat it, but they don't know how." We say that last line together.

"Smoke?" He hands me a cigarette. I don't smoke. "Me neither." I take it. He pulls another one out of the pack, lights that one, smokes. I just hold mine, study the crunchy bits of tobacco peeking out of the end of it. What a strange thing.

"Don't feel bad about Jackie," he says. "Shit happens." I don't feel bad. I'm jumpy. I've always been jumpy. She should know better than to put her hand on me without warning.

"I bet you're wild," he says. I pause.

No. Domestic, actually.

"Thoroughbred?"

Morgan, but I'm flattered.

"I thought Morgan horses were supposed to be chill." I can be chill. "You're chill, Eunice. I mean—" He blows smoke. It smells like how my owner Pete used to smell, and his wife Betty, and his son Junior. I don't know how Thomas can stand it, breathing in that smell.

"And no one knows that you're a horse?" They probably do. "I doubt it. I didn't know, until tonight." Really? "Yup. You're very good."

I should ask him about himself.

Are you thoroughbred? I regret asking as soon as the words leave my mouth. The question finally cracks him, breaks his face into the first real smile I've seen on him tonight, and his teeth are white, straight, short. Not unlike Tracy's.

"No, I'm not thoroughbred," he says.

"No need to say sorry," he says. "No, it's really okay."

Thomas finishes his stinky cigarette, tosses it onto the sidewalk to be with the rest of the trash breezing by. He digs in his pocket again. Another taxi pulls up. A man and a woman get out, head for the bright hotel doors.

"This hotel is nice, isn't it?" Yeah, you said that earlier. "I don't know why they gave me a king bed. I don't need all that space." From his pocket, he's pulled out a credit card. No, it's not a credit card. It's a hotel key. An extra one. Like the cigarette before, the one still in my hand, he holds it out to me.

"Room 826. Eighth floor. If you'd like some company after dinner."

I stare at the card in Thomas's perfectly delicate hand.

He is not a horse. He is a man who wants to have sex with a horse.

I'm looking forward to being by myself. As soon as possible. Thank you. He puts the card back in his pocket. "Understood."

Side-by-side we stand while he smokes. He checks his phone, runs his thumb on the screen. I crane my neck up to see where the top of the hotel meets the black sky. There are no stars out tonight. There might never be stars in the city. The hotel is the stars, white squares of windows in a grid, no twinkling.

Finally, Thomas turns back to the restaurant. "See you inside." Sure. "You're not leaving now, are you?" No. "Good." He disappears inside, and I'm alone again.

I look down the street, in the direction of where the cars and taxis are coming from. If I keep walking, I wonder, how far will I get until my walk breaks into a trot. A trot into a gallop, four legs working together as they do. They do still work, don't they? These legs are faster than these cars, because they don't follow their stop-and-go rules. I will run until the sidewalk breaks into a road, a road I will follow until it is no longer a road, but dirt and grass, and I will run back across all of it, across land and river and mud, westward to anywhere. Anywhere but here.

The city racket is suddenly cut with the clomp of shoes on pavement. The sound gets louder. A white horse hitched to a carriage turns the corner. Pulling three humans, he walks in front of the restaurant with neck swaying low. I try to keep my head down, look at the cigarette I'm holding, but as he gets close, I know that he must see me, recognize me for what I am. I smell him. He smells like horse. We exchange a glance as he passes, and in that glance we both know something about each other, envy something that the other has. He shakes his mane and keeps walking, holding his head a bit higher. I look around the city and am reminded of where I am. I can't run.

A breeze blows down the street. It blows the trash and causes all the coated humans to shiver, huddling inward and closer to each other on the sidewalk. The breeze smells like the restaurant, like seafood and salt, and I realize that I must be close to the ocean, closer than I've ever been in all my life. I think about all the fish in there, wonder what kinds there are, and how many. Do the humans catch the fish one by one, or do they catch them all at once as they swim together, too close to land? I should ask.

Show Hole

You respond to his message, noting the heavy scruff of his beard. Standard daddy. From the start, you're a little bored of the conversation; it's reminiscent of the hours you spent each day on AIM in high school, back when your screen name was MariahLuvr426. But he's hot and he's giving you attention:

Hey

Hey, how's it going?

Sup lol

Not much, just laying around in bed.
It's been a long day lol. How about you?

nm

Lol nice

After a few variations of this (he says "sup" at least two more times), he asks to trade nudes. You worked out earlier that day, you got a haircut, you're feeling good.

*If you say "no", turn to **PAGE 2**.*
If you send a full frontal while your chest and arms are freshly pumped and your
*hair is looking cute, turn to **PAGE 4**.*
*If you show hole, turn to **PAGE 8**.*

"Lol sorry, I'd rather not send pics," you tell him. He doesn't respond immediately and you feel it may seem odd that you're on a hook up app and aren't willing to send nudes.

You follow up with "It's just that I'd be fired if anyone at work saw I was on here. So I'd rather my pics not end up out in the world."

He doesn't respond.

You feel you should lighten it up, so you sprinkle in "haha [tongue out winky emoji]."

He still doesn't respond, but your texts aren't marked with a "Read" receipt yet. Your phone vibrates, indicating a new message from someone else on the app.

If you shoot your shot with this guy by sending him a "so horny"
*follow-up text, turn to **PAGE 3**.*
*If you move on to the next guy, turn to **PAGE 1**.*

You've been blocked.

This is how it always goes, isn't it? You knew you'd end up here. But your need to make a connection, to prove to yourself and even to that man that you *are* sexy and worth someone else's attention pushed him to a breaking point. You tried too hard. Maybe when the next one comes along you'll learn to control your spirals. Something to unpack with your therapist later.

Luckily for you, there's a bottle of wine and the whole wide world of Disney+ at your disposal.

If you turn on That's So Raven, ***END.***
If you take a chance with another guy, turn to ***PAGE 1.***

Thank god you cleaned your full-length mirror earlier, now is the time to put it to use. You tell him to hold on a minute, letting him know he's getting a personalized nude. He expresses his appreciation by responding with a purple smiling devil emoji.

You disrobe and pose in front of the mirror, phone at the ready, shifting your torso into various angles, making sure to flex hard enough so that he'll be impressed while maintaining a cool and casual air about it all. You're especially wary of the way you hold your phone when you take the mirror pic (your skinny wrists and long, piano-playing fingers are a point of self-consciousness). And what should you do with your face?

It takes roughly 30 takes, but you finally take a pic that you feel good about. You prepare to send it to him when you realize something...

You didn't clean your room. In the background of your nude, you can clearly see your desk chair which has accumulated a pile of unwashed clothes. Not to mention the floor around you is littered with all kinds of detritus.

There's nothing more unattractive to you than seeing a dirty room in a guy's nudes, but this is probably the best one you've ever taken.

If you send your nude anyway, turn to **PAGE 5**.
If you clean up a bit and do another 100 takes, turn to **PAGE 6**.

This is a quality nude, there's no denying it. You won't let this opportunity go to waste for a few weeks' worth of unwashed clothes. So you hit "send" and wait for a response.

"Damn, so hot," he says. You smile, injecting the compliment straight into your ego. You feel the sweet euphoria of serotonin in your bloodstream. Your dick hardens.

You begin typing a response, something along the lines of "let me see what I'm dealing with" but more sexy and less like you're in the mob asking him to show you the goods.

Before you can send it though, he shoots you another text.

"Lol is that a Celine Dion t-shirt behind you?"

And you freeze, the most prominent article of clothing is indeed a tee with Celine's face draped haphazardly over the back of your desk chair along with a mountain of clothing you've reminded yourself to wash at least twelve other times this week. Your mind calculates a number of scenarios. Is he turned off? Is it too feminine for him? Does he like it? Would he like to borrow it? Do you come across as one of "those gays"? Of all the things he could've pointed out, why was this the thing that drew his attention?

If you own it and tell him that it is indeed a Celine tee, turn to **PAGE 7**.
If you educate him on the toxicity of hyper-masculinity in the gay community, turn to **PAGE 3**.

The possibilities of this man being your potential future husband are slim (not that you'd even entertain the idea of marrying someone who considers "sup" as an acceptable conversation starter), but you have your own expectations to set and a reputation to uphold.

Potential future husband or no, this man with the beard will know what you're about and what you're about is an immaculate bedroom. You'll be rotting in hell before anyone sees the squalor.

So you toss your clothes into the darkest corner of your room, forming a smoldering meteor of cotton and polyester blends that are, at least, out of sight of your mirror.

You feel less confident about this new set of nudes and you make a note to do a leg day sometime soon.

"Cute," he replies. Unenthusiastic, maybe a tad uninterested. But "cute." You send him the purple devil face emoji.

That's how it begins. You direct him, telling him all the things you like. And he tells you all the things he wants to do to you, the positions he wants to get you in, he mentions choking you a little.

And when it's all done he has the audacity to ask you out for coffee or a drink. "Whichever you'd prefer," he offers.

If you'd prefer to sext and then ghost, turn to **PAGE 13** *to see the outcome.*
If you'd prefer coffee, turn to **PAGE 14** *to see the outcome.*
If you'd prefer a drink, turn to **PAGE 15** *to see the outcome.*

To suggest that "My Heart Will Go On" wasn't a monumental cultural shift would be homophobic, frankly. Even more so, to deny the impact of Celine Dion in your life would nearly be a hate crime and so you own up to the fact that, yes, you purchased a $65 T-shirt of her face from an Instagram ad when you were drunk and yes, you plan to frame it in a shadow box and hang it on your wall in memoriam when she dies.

The text thread goes silent. You can almost feel the life being sucked out of the conversation, leaving behind a chain of sup's and some bomb nudes.

You close out of the app and turn on your Disney+, prepared to watch *The Hunchback of Notre Dame* for the second time that day.

Then your phone vibrates and a notification appears at the top of your screen. He's sent you an image.

You open the app back up, dick grasped firmly in your hand, and there it is: It's an aerial shot taken from his neck down. His legs are bare, thighs chiseled like a couple of sledgehammers, and he's almost fully naked except for one thing.

A T-shirt bearing Celine Dion's face, pulled down just a bit to hide his dick. It looks to be older, a bit faded. Though you suppose that could speak to a poorer quality shirt. Nevertheless, it's the same T-shirt and you become lost in her eyes.

*Just fucking turn to **PAGE 11**.*

As a bottom, your ass is your greatest asset. And when you're selling that asset, it's important to highlight its most prominent feature—your asshole. The way you highlight your hole comes down to the quality of the angle from which you present it. You're not a novice to showing hole, but there is an art to it, and you hate how difficult it is to take a good holefie.

You know your options.

- **OPTION 1:** A typical mirror selfie except your back is towards the mirror and you have to twist your torso around while also spreading your ass with one hand. Opportunity for a coy, over-the-shoulder look.
- **OPTION 2:** On your back, legs held over your head, front-facing camera set and pointed at your hole like you're checking for hemorrhoids, which you've done before. Opportunity to catch your face straining to see the screen.

*If you choose **OPTION 1**, turn to **PAGE 9**.*
*If you choose **OPTION 2**, turn to **PAGE 10**.*

You pulled a muscle in your back trying to take this holefie. The position you placed yourself in coupled with the way you had to twist around to take the pic pinched a nerve or something. Regardless, you lay back in bed in complete pain after sending it. All that's left to do is wait for the response…

…which never comes.

You comb through the conversation looking for imperfections or more moments you have double texted or made a dumb joke that you'd only make around your closest friends; indicators of someone trying too hard to keep things moving. There's been nothing but nudes and sexting throughout, so what could've caused this man to ghost?

And that's when you notice it: your holefie. You notice the roll of fat on your lower back, emphasized by your horrible bedroom lighting. You notice the dimples in the middle of the fat. There's no doubt that this is what caused him to ghost. It's disgusting to look at, and now you're swiping through the pics you've posted on your profile.

The man you pretend to be on these hook-up apps is hot. He's interesting and well-read. There's some mysteriousness to him that you find attractive in other guys. But that's not the real you. The real you has a strained, toothy smile and is an open book, embarrassingly so. The real you has an oddly-shaped body that makes guys look the other way when they see it. The real you knows all the choreography from *High School Musical.*

Luckily for you, Disney+ has all three movies.

If you choose to masturbate to Zac Efron, **END***.*
If you choose to try again with another guy, turn to **PAGE 1***.*

You're terrified of yoga but somehow you've always been able to fold your body completely in half to take a picture of your asshole without so much as breaking a sweat. And here you are, on your back and bent at the waist with your arm and phone stretched below you to snap a pic of what your ex once called Marianas Trench. *Namaste.*

It's a good set of hole pics. You're not afraid to admit. It's practically art that deserves to be hung in the Louvre or MoMA. Whichever is less pretentious.

You hit "send" and he replies with three heart-eyed smiley face emojis.

"Yum. Take one more for me," he demands. This is Power you've only dreamed of obtaining, dangerous in the wrong hands. What will you do with it?

If you say "no" but push to continue sexting, turn to **PAGE 11**.
If you suggest he wait to see in person, turn to **PAGE 12**.

That's how it begins. You direct him, telling him all the things you like. And he tells you all the things he wants to do to you, the positions he wants to get you in, he mentions choking you a little. You feel in control, sexy.

And when you've both finished, he asks you out for coffee or a drink. "Whichever you'd prefer," he offers. You're not sure how sexts led to this, but you're certain the dynamic changed when you offered to buy him tacos after a good fuck.

Still...

*If you'd prefer to sext and then ghost, turn to **PAGE 13** to see the outcome.*
*If you'd prefer coffee, turn to **PAGE 14** to see the outcome.*
*If you'd prefer a drink, turn to **PAGE 15** to see the outcome.*

"Hell yeah, I'd be up for that. Let me take you out for a coffee or a drink, then you can come over afterwards and spend the night."

Despite them being the actual longest sentences he's typed in this conversation, it's not what you had in mind. What you had in mind was showing up at his place having spent the day fasting in order to prepare for the encounter. You imagined being freshly showered and gymed. Looking cute as hell. And you imagined him splitting you in half like a happy hour oyster until the break of day.

A date was something you had not prepared for. You can't imagine him being able to hold a conversation too far beyond "sup."

And yet...

*If you'd prefer to sext and then ghost, turn to **PAGE 13** to see the outcome.*
*If you'd prefer coffee, turn to **PAGE 14** to see the outcome.*
*If you'd prefer a drink, turn to **PAGE 15** to see the outcome.*

The year is 2052. Police and paramedics have responded to calls from neighbors complaining of a strange smell emitting from one of the apartments on their floor. What they find is a decomposed body laying in a king-sized bed. Naked except for a jock strap whose cup has been pushed to the side to reveal a sad-looking penis grasped by long, spindly fingers. The body's hand nearly completely severed from its arm right at its little, dainty wrist.

This is you. You spent the rest of your days utterly alone, jerking off three times a day until finally you just died while masturbating to *Mamma Mia 9: ABBA's Demise*. No known cause of death except that your heart simply gave out. A heart so weak and deteriorated from lack of attention. You knew no love. You framed a Celine Dion T-shirt in a shadow box and hung it on your wall.

Years later, the neighborhood children will tell ghost stories inspired by your life. They'll speak of a man whose soul left his body through his penis and now wanders the rooms of his abandoned apartment, moaning in that high pitched way like when you used to cum. They'll say if one enters the building and listens closely, one can hear the faint echoes of "Always Be My Baby" by Mariah Carey floating through the halls.

It's a sad tale. But it's your tale.

THE END.

You've found someone to love. Someone who appreciates you for everything that you are. Who sees the things that you don't like about yourself and embraces them. He takes the time to nurture and appreciate you and expects the same in return. You've never experienced anything more difficult or terrifying in your life than letting someone in and celebrating each other.

The two of you met at IKEA. You were shopping for a new full-length mirror after an unfortunate incident that your therapist told you not to dwell on too much. You opened up the app because it was IKEA and the options would most assuredly be endless. He was 21 feet away from you and you found him shopping for a new dresser which would not be practical enough for maintaining a clean room. Plus it was ugly, and you approached to let him know.

It took a while to get to this point and to this man. A few hundred dates, many nights crying, years of learning to be alone. But with each coffee date you've gone on, you've begun opening yourself up to the idea that you're deserving of this kind of love. Sure, there are times when you imagine the journey has brought you to this point for now, and dammit, you're happy with the way things are going.

As for the man from the story, you never saw him again after that first coffee date. He had a weird mole on his neck.

THE END.

You're single, and thank God for that.

Your last relationship ended when you proved to the guy you were dating that you knew all the choreography from the *High School Musical* franchise and he texted you the next day saying that your interpretation of "Bet On It," which isn't even real choreography, lacked any emotional depth or conflict. You were done being disappointed by men.

You began therapy, started traveling. You blacked out at pub karaoke in Dublin one night and sang "Always Be My Baby" by Mariah Carey while Mariah herself, unbeknownst to you, sat in the back of the room. The duet that transpired went viral and the two of you appeared on Ellen together. You're now living off a portion of Mariah's royalties.

This is the life you never knew you wanted. There's something freeing about being by yourself. You're alone but never lonely because the experiences that have come out of it have been valuable and healing. Your time being single has taught you so much more about yourself than you ever thought you knew. It's brought you the sort of love that you felt you always deserved.

And money. Lots of money.

THE END.

An Interview with Damitri Martinez

Foglifter contributor Zak Salih's new novel *Let's Get Back to the Party* is a glittery, gay account of two men navigating through the complex arrays of marriage, sex, and friendship. But more than just a queer ode, the novel is also deeply concerned with our capacity to heal, and how the passage of time gives us opportunities to reconcile difficult relationships from our past. At the end of January, I had the chance to speak with Zak, where he provided more inspiring insights about his approach to the novel.

Damitri Martinez (DM): First of all it was such a pleasure reading the book. I just loved that it was for gay men, and I just thank you so much for putting it out there for gay men.

Zak Salih (ZS): I'm happy to hear you say that, because there was a lot of pressure in the early stages of writing this novel. You're obviously taking upon yourself a huge responsibility when you write, even a work of fiction, about a marginalized group. In the initial planning stages of this novel, I felt this immense pressure, because gay male community is in itself just so incredibly diverse, to encompass every single perspective.

The real key to writing this book came when I just let go of that responsibility. I don't think it's a writer's responsibility to carry the burden of an entire community, on their shoulders, specifically because there's absolutely no way a single sustained work of fiction could encompass every single gay man's perspective and experience, let alone that of the larger queer community.

Absolved of that responsibility, I could make Oscar and Sebastian as sad and as angry and misunderstood and hypocritical as I wanted to, because, first and foremost, they're not just gay men, they're human, regardless of what groups they identify with. While this book is unapologetically intended for gay men, I hope it speaks to as many people as possible. I myself have other interests, including how people cope with the passing of time—something that's not exclusive to gay men or even to queer people.

DM: I like what you're saying about absolving yourself of feeling like you had to write for the entire community. It allows you to really get into the specific struggles and complexities and idiosyncrasies of characters, which are written really authentically in this book. I do want to say though, when I was reading Oscar and Sebastian, I felt like these two characters, they were both incredible forces, they felt so much bigger, almost like these queer archetypes and the characterization felt really powerful. What went into developing these two characters?

ZS: Archetypes, I hope. Stereotypes, no. I mean, if you think of the gay male experience as a spectrum, it's fairly obvious from the beginning of the novel that Oscar and Sebastian sit on the ends of two extremes. There's definitely a huge gap of experience and understanding between the two of them. I was curious to see what would happen if you put these extremes in opposition to one another. And again, I had to be very careful because you obviously don't want to make any blanket statements, like "All all gay men want to get married," or "All gay men just want to fuck all the time." But for the sake of the story I was trying to tell, I think having two characters that kind of embodied that experience was all the drama and all the narrative thrust I needed to write the book.

DM: Yes, definitely. And I don't want to make it seem like these characters are two dimensional, in any way, because I think there're so many answers in the book where the main characters, they need some sort of compassion, not just from readers, but from other characters, it looks like they're seeking compassion from others.

ZS: Right, right. They're looking for something in each of their—I guess for lack of a better term—intergenerational foils, right? Sebastian is looking for something in his student, Arthur, and Oscar is looking for something in the writer, Sean, and they spend so much time obsessing over this. I mean, Sean has made a career of being a sort of gay ethnographer and writing these passages that Oscar finds very titillating. But he also ends up getting married. There's a larger discussion to be had: You think about the people in our own lives that we objectify or obsess over, and you're never seeing the whole picture. You're only getting fragments, and that's why these people end up disappointing us in one way or another. Not because they're bad people butt because they're human. There will always be a part of them that is unknown and unknowable.

DM: I really love how you lift up the vulnerability of these characters. I feel so compassionate towards them, you know? And I just really love what we're actually dealing with are these two men who are so vulnerable. What you do so well, is lift up their vulnerability, as they look for each other in different characters. But that does make me wonder: With these two being on opposite ends of the spectrum, and you suggesting they need each other, do you think they're good for each other?

ZS: [*Laughs*] Uh...no, Damitri, I don't. Nevertheless, they need to come to terms with one another as a way of moving on. There's this beautiful quote by the writer Rebecca Solnit where she says, "The art is not in forgetting but in letting go." They need to let go of one another, but I don't think that requires having to forget one another.

DM: When I read queer literature, whether intentional or not, I always have this question in the back of my mind where I'm like, How should gay men love? I'm always looking for a representation of good love, you know what I mean?

ZS: Yeah, yeah, yeah. But I never really thought of this novel as a love story. I was more interested in the friendship angle. The thrust of this novel was never about, Are they going to fall in love, are they going to be in a relationship, are they going to get married? Those stories are wonderful, of course. . But in the case of Oscar and Sebastian, it felt a little too simplistic. I'm in my late 30s, and I've been in a relationship for almost 10 years now, and I think back to when I was in my 20s and how preoccupied I was with things like like sex and romance; now, I'm more interested in the concept of friendship. That, to me, is so much more interesting. So it was never a question of whether Oscar and Sebastian were going to fall in love. It's, How are they going to navigate these gaps in their understanding of the world, and what does that mean for their potential to be friends, or to not be friends at all?

DM: I didn't want to pigeonhole this as a love story, because I don't think it's that at all. I think part of the tension, though, is how are these people actually trying to make themselves whole? Not just love for someone else, but the love for self that you have to establish first, which I think was really emphasized and really beautiful in your book.

ZS: That's a great way to put it. Therein is the essence of pride, right? It's really about how you feel about yourself when you're alone in a room. I could go to all the parties, and get laid all the time, but if I'm in a room by myself, and I hate myself, I would argue that I probably don't have a healthy level of pride. I mean, the project of pride is communal, but I think the more important work, at least in my experience as a gay man, is that no one can help you with that but yourself. This is something that I kind of flirted with in the novel, this idea of being a part of a community but also needing (or feeling) set apart from that community. We need each other to survive, but there are certain things you can only do by yourself. One of them, I think, is cultivating a truly authentic sense of pride.

DM: Yes, and in a marginalized community that's had to create our own examples of pride and love, it's hard to go out there and be proud or self-loving. I think something else I appreciated in your book is how you've incorporated these characters that serve as mentors, especially in these very human mentorships, because they're not perfect. In fact, sometimes they're anger-inducing, and sometimes awkward, especially when you watch the relationship between Arthur and Sebastian. I'm just wondering if that was intentional on your part.

ZS: It absolutely was. The idea was to ground the experience of Oscar and Sebastian in this kind of continuity of gay history. There's this kind of solipsistic idea of feeling like you're always the present, and you forget there are people who came before you, and people coming after you whose experiences are incredibly different from your own.. A lot of that was drawn from my own feelings about what it means to be a member of a generation suspended between two completely different experiences of living as a gay man. The ideal relationship is that these mentors are here to teach you—but what happens when you envy them, when you get lost in this idea that they've lived (or are living) a more authentic life than yours?

Years and years ago, there was a YouTube clip of this older gay gentleman—he must have been in his late 60s—and a teenage boy, and they were sitting on a stage across from one other talking about their experiences as gay. It was delightfully heartwarming and inspiring. But I also remember thinking, Man, if I were this old man confronted with this boy, there would be a part of me embittered by how easy this boy has it compared to me. That's obviously not a very generous thought, but those subterranean feelings and emotions you're not proud to articulate are often the wellspring for an interesting story.

DM: I love that, because it really does capture the timelessness of that bumpy transfer of knowledge. I'm thinking about how it's laid out in your novel, because you have Sean, who is the oldest of them, with Oscar looking at Sean, and he's envying the nostalgia of whatever Sean's life was, and then you have Sebastian looking at Arthur, envying the freedom of youth.

ZS: I'm so glad you latched on to that. But it's also, to use the cliche, like they're looking at it through rose-tinted glasses. Oscar obviously objectifies the experiences Sean has had. But Oscar's problem, to me, is that he has no respect for the past. He's objectifying all this sex and not paying much credence to the more serious experiences of Sean's generation. So you have someone like Oscar, who couldn't be bothered to care about the past, and then you have someone like Sebastian, who cares way too much for it.

DM: Well, you know, I *did* have a favorite character—I know you were trying to balance—

ZS: Oh! Well, who was it? I mean, I know, I'm supposed to love all my characters equally, and parents aren't supposed to pick favorites—but they do. And I have a favorite. So I'm curious, who was it?

DM: Sebastian had my heart the whole way through. There's just something about him that resonates. He's who I felt I could pay homage to, with my art obsession, my sensitivity, my desire for the picturesque...

ZS: I'm Team Sebastian as well. That being said, I'm always fascinated by unsavory characters? So writing about Oscar, who is someone, for me at least, so far removed from my experience, was a real treat. I so enjoyed his acerbic tone, and we all know a guy like Oscar.

DM: Some of us *date* guys like Oscar...

ZS: [*laughs*] I remember in the early drafts—and this led to the final structure of the book—I would write in Sebastian's voice and then get tired of it and then write in Oscar's voice, and then need a break from him. I kept oscillating between these two very different experiences and tones and voices. And I it ended up working perfectly. There were a lot of exciting things that emerged in the editing.

DM: You can feel that authentic balance when you're reading, and it really is helpful to be in one mindset and then switch completely into the other for this story. You can feel it authentically, you can feel the narrative organically grow between the two of them.

ZS: Yeah, thanks. You switch from one perspective, and it's like you're taking a breath. Because as much as I love these men, they're so immersed in their anger and their sadness that they admittedly run the risk of coming across as pills. But because you have that breathing space, it made the emotions more manageable, and it opened up opportunities either to engineer or, in most instances, to discover by happenstance, the ways in which their respective voyages kind of mirror one another, or play off of one another.

DM: One of the other things I really loved about Sebastian and the way that you wrote him was how you framed his thoughts and scenes with portraiture and visual art. I thought it was just so beautiful. I wondered if you had a strong passion for the visual arts and if it was something you were trying to honor for yourself as an author, or was it just something that was for the character alone.

ZS: I do have a passion for visual art, for sure. But outside of one art history class I took as a general education course in college, I have no academic background in it. I'm coming at it purely as just someone who loves pretty pictures.

DM: You wrote as if you were a professor!

ZS: [*laughs*] Thanks! In terms of the ekphrastic passages, I had so much fun writing them. I wasn't convinced an entire novel could have been written "ekphrastically," but that was a very central idea of how Sebastian sees his world and just how prevalent the past is on his mind, that he cannot look at a work of art without being reminded in some way about his personal history. I suspect that's true of any of us who look at a photograph or a painting or a sculpture. I mean we're seeing it, on one level, as the artist intended, but you always bring something of yourself to it, and so those passages with Sebastian were a dramatization of how much we personalize the experience of looking at a work of art. It seemed a sensible way for him to incorporate the past, without resorting to the device of pure flashback.

DM: No, it was beautiful. There was like something very poetic about it and especially—again no spoilers—but how you incorporate that final scene with Oscar into what we see with Sebastian…

So we can't ignore the important backdrop of your novel: the Supreme Court ruling of same sex marriage. I remember when I first heard about it, I was elated, I was like, Yes this is great! I'm so excited! And then when I was completing my master's, I came across this paper by Judith

Butler that just ripped apart same sex marriage, saying that this is just another political ploy by heteronormative culture to pull us into the center and in total defiance of what queer culture is all about. It was really exciting to see some of those debates played out in the novel. The novel isn't promoting one view or the other, I'll say that, and I think it was really interesting to see the characters maneuver and incorporate this historic backdrop into their lives. Why did you choose to make that so central to the novel?

ZS: The setting came into place on a random day when I was thinking about the timeframe for this novel. To me, it was this kind of very horrible synchronicity that, in June of 2015, you had the Supreme Court ruling and this moment of public celebration, a sense of victory, and almost exactly a year later, you had the Pulse nightclub shooting, this moment of very public communal trauma. Both moments shaped the queer community to a very severe extent. There was something about making that year a kind of laboratory in which to study how Oscar and Sebastian live their lives. When you look at it in light of what came after that Supreme Court ruling (not just the Pulse nightclub shooting but the four years after, with the Trump administration and the rollbacks on civil rights) , there's a dramatic irony at play. The reader knows, to some extent, where this story is headed, and it casts a shadow over everything.

DM: Something I considered to be a really great plot device was the hookup culture technology. And I thought that your use of a "Cruze" is a cool literary display, sort of like Shakespeare's letters. An important event that happened with Sebastian happened because of this piece of technology. It just reminded me of a scene in a Shakespeare play where we're like, "Oh my god, they read the letter, now what!?"

ZS: Wow, that's great. I never thought of it that way. I mean I think most people who've been on those apps, regardless of whether they live in a city or a small town, have invariably run into someone they've seen on there, either at a distance or in some kind of awkward close encounter. These awkward encounters are facilitated by apps that, on the one hand, have made connecting among gay men so much easier, but also shows our ability to trivialize and commodify people. And I don't say this as a judgment on the project of recreational sex—but in my experience with these apps, it just makes it so much easier to treat people as disposable, and I don't think there's anything to be proud of in that.

DM: You kind of see that in Oscar's character. He's gotten used to just sort of "clicking" on people. He doesn't want to think deeply about anything, about the past, he doesn't want to think about any of that. And so it's sort of like he's condensed himself into one of those little profile boxes.

ZS: Yeah, and in a strange way, the gallery of pictures on his phone is a kind of digital art gallery when put into contrast with the artworks Sebastian looks at all the time. Both men are obsessed, on some level, with images in frames.

DM: I'm starting to see it more and more in stories, these hook-up apps, and I honestly felt like it was an actual device in your book, and I thought it was done so well, whether it was intended, or not.

ZS: This is the challenge of writers nowadays. We either have to retreat to a time before this technology and tell our stories there, or we have to find ways to incorporate it into the stories we tell about the present.

DM: I know your novel is about to make its debut, but what's next? Are you working on anything else?

ZS: I have a couple projects I've been working on for some time, so I'm glad to have those as I take off my writer hat and become "the author" and put myself out in the world. It's nice to have those projects to keep me busy, because when this is all over I at least won't have to sit in front of a blank computer screen. Regardless of how incomplete it is, there will be something there to help me get my bearings.

DM: Just thinking about how you're talking, I've had the pleasure of reading your short stories, a couple of them, as well as the novel, and your style is very versatile. Do you have like a novel hat that you wear while you're writing a novel, and then switch it when you're writing short stories?

ZS: Yes, I picked it up at the grocery store, but I'm sure you can find it anywhere. [*laughs*] No, no, that's a really good question, and certainly one I think about. The way I approach it is: the style and form has to match the story one is trying to tell. I don't think this novel could have been written the way that I wrote "A Life of Its Own" [published in Volume 5, Issue 2 of *Foglifter*]—or vice versa. And from a purely selfish standpoint: It just makes things more interesting for me as a writer. It's an opportunity to exercise different muscles. One of the exciting things about short story collections is that you get to see such an interesting range of d styles, but also a throughline. A singular voice. I think of Carmen Maria Machado's *Her Body and Other Parties*. The collection is so dynamic, yet at no point did I feel as if any particular story was written by someone other than Machado.

DM: You know, I wanted to add, because I do want to promote your Instagram account, because you're always posting what you're reading and you have impeccable taste in literature. How do you let reading influence your own writing?

ZS: Oh, thank you for saying that. I have no academic training in writing. Everything I learned about writing, and have yet to learn, comes from writing, but more importantly, from reading. There really is nothing else one needs to do but read and write in order to become a writer. If you have the means to join an MFA program, I think that's great. The one thing I regret about not having participated in an MFA program is that I have to go out there and forge a community of writers on my own. Like tapping the shoulders of strangers at a party and saying, Hey, can I join the conversation? I imagine there's a vibrant feeling of community that comes from an MFA program that you can't get from just reading and writing by yourself. Reading, though, is why I wanted to do this to begin with. If I had to choose between writing and reading, I would quit writing tomorrow. And just read.

Aubade with Jackfruit

at this hour, i ungum myself from you only when necessary.
there is a knock at the door. there is an organ demanding
sweet release. our sheets, sap in their folds, sponge up
around two liters of salted water between us in the preceding
hours. more or less depending on whether or not we wake
knee-to-knee and how long the heating pad spent lullabying
at your back and how many of my prescribed thirteen daily gems
have been laying claim to me lately. lugging around a body defiant
of being lugged gives morning breath and eau de precociousness.
maybe you rub lotion into where my skin is splitting before i go
to boil the oats. maybe i time our waking against the lost sleep.
measure twice, cut once. but today is the day the woman at the store
said our treasure would be sweet enough for the slaughter,
the fruit that could have reminded us of home, had home been
made for us under different circumstances. had our fathers chosen
motherland over our mothers. the woman doing the selling, perhaps
sharing a tongue with you beyond that which is eager for a fruited
milk sweet and sticky, envelope glue nectar. the enormity of this
scaled carapace has no business being in our kitchen, in this
country, but we forgive ourselves, this once, for the washed
and hung ziplocs, the period panties, the kale seedlings growing
on our sill. an indulgence, an event, a savoring, because and in spite
of the ways our bodies fail us and we, them. for once, i cleaver
a skull and bring a bread knife across its brainstem. for once,
your hands separate and pile: seed fat, sinew pith, goldripe muscle.

let the rest of the day be our repentance, let us piously hydrate.
this now, you feed flesh into me like you never have before.

ANTHONY AGUERO

I Was

I was
in a big house,
full moon,
directionless
but I was safe.
And the birds.

There was a fluttering in the chest
but it was teeth falling down a flight
of stairs mistaken for a case of wings.

I was
in a big house,
many rooms,
no stars, &
assumed safety.
And the hands.

The mangoes were ripe and a thief
stole all but one sweet, plump infant
right from the branches of his tree.

I was
in a big house,
no rooms,
many lights, &
my breathing.
And the murder.

To de-feather a bird one must first
kill. So they killed the bird. A million
birds fell from the empty night sky.

I was
in a big house,
full moon,
like a ripe melon.
Many rooms,
let me keep you
safe. Go, run.

JASMINE SAWERS

Domestic Curses for All Occasions

Did you lock the door? Did you turn the oven off?

Picture this: A careless man, someone who has tossed out your heart like so much chaff, is beset by a creeping worry. *I'm sorry, I have to check my house,* he'll say ten minutes into a date. *I think something's wrong,* he'll tell his boss in the middle of a meeting. He's back and forth between his home and his life, and that home swallows him whole.

Not dazzling enough for you? Look, you can't go big with a curse. Rather, you can't discount the impact of going small. We're not giving people pestilent boils or snatching up firstborns here, man. Don't be fucking crass. Go to the mall if you want that kind of thing. You came to me because I'm an artist. This isn't Die Hard 9. This is *Dreams*, and I'm Kurosawa.

You won't be able to escape the clutter.

Say you've got yourself a collector. What does she love? Books and journals and calligraphy pens? She can't walk through her wealth of them. Computers and tablets and monitors? They cascade in her wake, and they'd shatter but for the cushion of detritus on her floor. Clothes and shoes and handbags? She's trapped, suffocating beneath the mountain of all she has—strictly metaphorically, of course.

There is a draft. But where from?

It shivers down the walls and whistles through her skin. *It's an old house,* she'll say. Or: *my father, bless him, did the insulation.* She'll hunt for it, casually at first, but her urgency increases with time. She'll not eat, she'll not sleep. All the furniture, all her books, all her pots and pans and plates and glasses—she'll gather them in the center of each room so she can best monitor the windows, the doors, the cabinets for mouseholes and pinholes and daylight through the rafters. Her eyes become razors. Her fingers become talons.

Your dog will find you tedious.

This is for someone who has never loved a lover more than he loves his dog. He breaks up with anyone who sneezes at dog hair on the furniture. He reheats pasta from a can so he can afford for the dog to eat raw gourmet. He's moved across the country and back with her head in his lap all the while. He can't sleep unless he can hear her snoring beside him.

He tells her all his secrets. *You're the only one who loves me, Butternut. There must be something essentially wrong deep inside me, Butternut. I'm a monster, Butternut.*

One day, she heaves a great sigh, and turns away.

You will lose the words, "thank you."

Perhaps you know a busy mom. She's booked from the first shock of the alarm at six until her kids tumble out of the minivan after the game, the cello lessons, the extra math tutoring. The first time she chokes, it's in front of the barista at her favorite coffee joint, then it's her own mother, dropping off this week's casserole. Her niece, babysitting on a Saturday night, and then her neighbor, rescuing her trash cans from where they were blown in the street. The school counselor, who calls with an opportunity for her eldest, and then her husband, who tells her to relax while he goes to the parent-teacher meeting.

Her tongue is parched and the words become dust she coughs up. Everyone she loves turns to stone before her.

You will think of me every day.

I don't think this one's for you. This is for the discerning client more interested in results than theatrics. This is for someone who need not see to know.

Because a good curse, a *real* curse, begins in love. People don't come to me because they have an annoying coworker, or a neighbor who has loud parties. The price is too high for that. You come to me because love's got you in tatters. You show up here and you say, *ah, my ex-wife is vain,* and I distort all her mirrors. *Oh, my boyfriend watches TV while I clean up after him and the kids all my days,* and I turn him into an obsessive tormented by stray flecks of dirt. *Dear me, my mother doesn't know how to love,* and I give her a mother's heart with no one to exercise it on. But no one ever asks me, *Arda, how did you get here?*

There was a girl, and I loved her more than she loved me. She loved herself so well that there was nothing left for anyone else. For her I split myself open, I carved myself inside out, I lobbed my only wish out into the ether, oblivious to anything listening: *I hope you think of me every day.*

I have heard she's thrice-divorced. I have heard her children do not visit her at home. I have answered the phone only to hear her breath come heavy down the line before she hangs up.

I have sat alone in the light of the waning moon, sipping up my success.

Anyway, tell me: who is it that's worth your heart?

After John Edmonds' *Untitled (New Haven), 2015*

"In moonlight, black boys look blue."
—Juan, Moonlight (2016)

having once been blue myself,
I now pay attention
to the skeletons of the lights. the way

rays of almost-gold can bend,
sharpen and cut away at the darkness;
the way the darkness can hold

inside it the possibility for all color. for
all touch. for once, I want to be held,
and I want it to mean something

outside of the moment we could be
suspended in—such sensational light
cracked into the most delicate geometry,

draped over the valleys of our hips like
a body consumed by white satin sheets. like every-
thing bright, this, too, is temporary

joy. the feeling is: a false sun challenging
our deepest contours, and I am still cold when
we touch. it is just like I said,

once I was blue, and now I feel everything. I
am releasing my cooler, heavier hues. I am leaving
more room for imagination; I am building a

new world from the amber tint the morning casts
for us around my room. maybe, the world
is not what is new, but the warmth—the warmth

of hands without the heat; the warmth of flesh
without the expectation of its splitting into
its options. or, just the palette livening. the red

under my skin interrupting this artificial
landscape. the difference in feeling is
how much color I am willing to bleed.

RaJon Staunton

Pantoum for Black Boyhood

"O little root of a dream / you hold me here / undermined
by blood, / no longer visible to anyone…"
—Paul Celan, "O Little Root of a Dream"

what more can be said about the sand? its covering
of a personal archive made by the lull of the tide? my mouth
misremembers salt water. sea breeze. blood moon eclipsed by clouds
that last fourth of July we spent buried in the grit of fireworks.

of a personal archive made by the lull of the tide, my mouth
is full. of the broken hymns of summertime, my ears are not sure.
that last fourth of July we spent buried in the grit of fireworks
unspools like a dream. the shoreline releases its seam,

is full of the broken hymns of summertime. my ears are not sure.
I am trying to imagine an uncharted closeness. my proximity to joy
unspools like a dream. the shoreline releases its seam.
as if in a movie: the credits roll. the horizon draws my silhouette against the waves.

I am trying to imagine an uncharted closeness: my proximity to joy,
the distance between the beginning and the end of a memory.
as if in a movie, the credits roll; the horizon draws my silhouette against the waves.
let heaven be the moment I rediscover innocence, let it be

the distance between the beginning and the end of a memory—
the last time I slept with the balcony door open, let the grainy air rock me.
let heaven be the moment I rediscover innocence. let it be
my mama's arms in '14, wrapped around my shoulders like a promise.

the last time I slept with the balcony door open—let the grainy air rock me—
I misremembered salt water, sea breeze, blood moon swallowed by clouds;
my mama's arms in '14, wrapped around my shoulders like a promise.
what more can be said about the sand? its covering?

RAJON STAUNTON

Chiron and I Consider Violence

after *Moonlight (2016)*

everything in this life feels
like a bruise reopened

into its wound. I've never
been in a real fight, but watching

you, I can feel the ghost of it
in my bones: honey-covered knuckles,

blows landing like heartbeats
booming, cracking the pavement.

and it's just that easy to get lost
in the differences between desire

and something hungrier
with sharper, blood-dipped teeth.

let me admit, Chiron, I am afraid to face
the duality of my own hands—the way they clasp

around prayer and curl into my rage,
almost purely embody its unchambered heat—but

this is the only way we know how
to want anything new: a rustling and then

streams of static through the ears, mouthfuls
of blood pouring over teeth like warm wine; with

fingers coiled around my neck,
or a head buried in your deepened chest

years later, fists opened over your heart—digging
through you to find the lull of a familiar ocean.

MARY ANGELINO

Practicing Motherhood

At twelve the rabbits were mine—
their hutches abandoned
fairgrounds, the air before lightning.

I folded lettuce through the wires,
they ate and leapt away in seconds
but the feeling stayed like smoke

from candles on a cake—skywriting
I caught just before it disappears.
At night I'd sneak out to that wild

thrashing—a flash of coyote? Just stillness,
the yard holding its breath. But one night
I chose sleep instead. That morning—

eyedropper for a bottle, milk-soaked
bread, a shoebox and an old dishrag
for the one who survived—

my sleeping thumb, my fitful twitch—
panic stills if you press it gently
to your chest, to warmth
and slow breaths.

excerpt from Untitled

while snowing, a
man was shot by
police. the news
explained in great
detail that cops tried
not to shoot, that
they let him back
officers down the
block, asking and
asking and asking
him to drop his
knife, "imploring"
—that's their word
for this sharp
nagging at tense. a
begbeggedbegging
issue. they shot him
3 times. they rushed
to the hospital. with
him. and no. no,
i don't want this
for us. i don't want
this shit anymore.
tired of desperate
needs to arm
myself.
i wish there was less
of this, less
begging! listen to
me: i could never
own a gun! i want
less fear in my
search. less terrors
to imagine, held up
to our own knowl-
edge edge of what
happens. and no. no,
no he wasn't

.and voluntarily, police shot and killed a Black man
who was mentally ill while his mother was trying
to deescalate her son and the police. guard my love
like a mother but i'm unfit to mother. insane Black
and painful. difficult to read. being of sound mind,
willfully..

.and voluntarily, police shot and killed a Black man who was mentally ill while his mother was trying to deescalate her son and the police. guard my love like a mother but i'm unfit to mother. insane Black and painful. difficult to read. being of sound mind, willfully...and voluntarily, police shot and killed a Black man who was mentally ill while his mother was trying to deescalate her son and the police. guard my love like a mother but i'm unfit to mother. insane Black and painful. difficult to read. being of sound mind, willfully...and voluntarily, police shot and killed a Black man who was mentally ill while his mother was trying to deescalate her son and the police. guard my love like a mother but i'm unfit to mother. insane Black and painful. difficult to read. being of sound mind, willfully...and voluntarily, police shot and killed a Black man who was mentally ill while his mother was trying to deescalate her son and the police. guard my love like a mother but i'm unfit to mother. insane Black and painful. difficult to read. being of sound mind, willfully...and voluntarily, police shot and killed a Black man who was mentally ill while his mother was trying to deescalate her son and the police. guard my love like a mother but i'm unfit to mother. insane Black and painful. difficult to read. being of sound mind, willfully...and voluntarily, police shot and killed a Black man who was mentally ill while his mother was trying to deescalate her son and the police. guard my love like a mother but i'm unfit to mother. insane Black and painful. difficult to read. being of sound mind, willfully...and voluntarily, police shot and killed a Black man who was mentally ill while his mother

was trying to deescalate her son and the police.
guard my love like a mother but i'm unfit to
mother. insane Black and painful. difficult to read.
being of sound mind, willfully...and voluntarily,
police shot and killed a Black man who was
mentally ill while his mother was trying to deesca-
late her son and the police. guard my love like a
mother but i'm unfit to mother. insane Black and
painful. difficult to read. being of sound mind

JAMAL RASHAD

Confessional Poem #6

If there's a stain on the couch then its my stain
and it's my couch. I hold a mirror up to myself
to ask questions. This is another kind of mapping.
I run the free hand loose up and down
my stomach and I wonder when was the last time
I allowed myself the privilege of a meal.
Lately I've made a habit of swallowing stones
before my showers and leaving the meat out.
I've gone days without speaking and called it spiritual.
I've gone days without work and called it a new life.
When my old man calls from down the hall for an odd suck
I tell him that I've missed my delivery of Newsweek
and that he'll have to wait till I get the time.

JAMAL RASHAD

Auguries

a crumb of dumb
a knock of salt
a puff of smoke
a vote of choice

a stroke of chalk
a sound of spit
a hum of him
a sigh of course

a pinch of sand
a feel of wood
a laugh of sun
a smoke of meat

a bit of care
a piece of snatch
a dab of paint
a gift of kiss

a pound of sound
a wink of chance
a strain of blood
a nod of voice

a flash of teeth
a blues of cum
a buck of spring
a thumb of drank

a side of squeal
a room of chest
a inch of man
a life of skirts

a grab of mad
a bite of green
a quart of suck
a stem of stomp

a splash of bo
a drip of horse
a chew of rib
a view of home

Tauheed Zaman

The Desert Spirit

When I was six years old, my father lifted me on his shoulders to kiss a meteorite. We stood in a vast courtyard, its marble floor cool under our feet. Twin minarets rose into the desert sky. It was 1989, and I didn't know the word "pilgrimage" yet. But when he lifted me above the crowd of white-robed thousands, I knew that we were standing at the center of the center of the center of our universe.

My parents taught me three stories about the meteorite at the Great Mosque of Mecca. The most scientific explanation was that it burned through the atmosphere to land in the Arabian Peninsula thousands of years ago. This explained the black color of the rock, which so awed the Bedoin tribes that they passed it down for generations. The city grew among the dunes and the meteorite became a fixture of the mosque. Today, millions of pilgrims travel each year to circle the stone in its courtyard and wait in line to press their lips to its dark surface. We are all one tribe, re-enacting the desert raves of our spiritual ancestors.

The religious stories were far more fantastic. One maintained that the meteorite was a divine marker, guiding the prophet Mohammad to the site of his first and holiest mosque. Another claimed that the rock was more ancient still, carried by Adam and Eve from the gardens of heaven. The stone, like its couriers, was the worse for wear. It started a celestial white and ended its journey an earthly black, as it absorbed the sins of the world. Both legends agreed firmly on one point, however: the stone could still absorb and absolve sins. All you had to do was brave the desert journey, cast aside all doubt, and kiss the rock like your afterlife depended on it.

With these tales, my mother convinced my father to make the pilgrimage. She was more elated still when, after a long trip to the Great Mosque, my father said, "we might as well," and carried me towards the meteorite waiting line. We parted the circling worshippers. Those too old or too weak to push through the crowds stood and pointed towards the stone instead, muttering prayers from a distance. Everyone wore white robes like ours. I passed concentric circles of raised index fingers and wondered if they were all showing us the way.

I wondered why my mother had hugged me tight before my father carried me into the crowd. I wonder that still. Had she felt joy? Relief? Had she breathed a sigh, shut her eyes, and imagined that something within her son, something small and blooming and as persistent as a desert weed, would soon be put right? Or perhaps she hugged me out of fear, out of premonition.

Perhaps she knew I would never kiss the stone.

When my father raised me to the meteorite, I clutched his shoulders in wonder. It was embedded in a ring of silver plating, shining maroon-dark and concave at the center. The murmurs of the crowd drowned out my father's instructions. I leaned towards the stone, lost my balance, and the world seemed to tilt. I rocked forward and hit my forehead on its hard surface. The sting spread through my skull as I bounced backward, then gripped desperately with my legs to stay upright. I had the panicked thought that I had done it wrong and reached towards the rock to try again.

But already we were turning away. Already my father was lowering me back to the ground. Already he was leading me back past the pointing fingers, over the cool tiles, to where my mother waited at the edge of the crowd, dressed in white and smiling.

As a teenager, I became convinced that I had head-butted the meteorite. That my small, brown body had recoiled and refused to brush my lips against the relic. But for this protective reflex, I thought, religion might have slipped past my lips and to my child-heart, settled deep in its den, a mongoose around a snake. It might have snuffed out my curiosity, my laughter, my queerness. It was 1998, and I had just come out to my best friend in high school. Thank goodness, she said, that I left the desert with the stone unkissed. Thank goodness, I added, that we emigrated to a snowy corner of America, where desert fables could fade behind us.

My parents questioned my jaunty atheism at first. In their minds, the meteorite legends and scientific explanations still lived comfortably side-by-side like encyclopedias on the shelf, congruent and equally true. I laughed and told them that space stones had no effect on me, Mecca, or on the universe. As the years passed, my father drifted with me towards skepticism. My mother donned a hijab and delved deeper into her Qur'an. And yet the two balanced each other out perfectly, living in suburban harmony.

I moved out. I came out. I went away to college, came out again, and went to more school. Each loop of the gyre took me farther. Each journey felt like a magnification of that first turn away from the stone. I breathed easier, danced harder, got a graduate degree, and a lot of tattoos along the way.

Tattoos of course, were haraam—forbidden—so sinful, my mother reminded me, that I could never be buried in a Muslim cemetary, or granted admission to heaven. A permanent disqualification by ink. I told her heaven sounded like an Ivy League school, and that I didn't mind being out of the running. My father drove me to the airport, looked me up and down, and patted my arm.

"No more, please," he said. "You'll get hepatitis."

In San Francisco, I was disheartened when my body twisted away from more than just religion. It recoiled from the easy intimacy I saw all around me. It was 2016. I spent my days finishing graduate school and nights searching for the divine on different dance floors.

My favorite was at the Stud, a joyful dive the size of a shoe box. The bathroom stalls were doorless, the coat check dimly lit. Printed signs above the bar proudly stated "We Have Narcan—Just Ask." I loved everything about the place, but especially Saturday nights, when the speakers blared deep cuts of disco hits. This brought brown and black and beige bodies spilling onto the dance floor. I always wore a plain shirt, but orbited friends who wore flowing kaftans, and tuxedos, and wigs, and leather harnesses, and gold eye shadow. They snapped Chinese fans against the heat. I watched as men brushed thighs and hips. As they kissed and laughed and kissed again. My own legs buzzed electric, ready to send me curving between strangers, to make contact. But I always fought it, that elliptical longing.

Then at one end of the room the owner would raise a spotlight to the mirrorball. I would feel the weight of the desert drain briefly from my shoulders, and sing along.

When we get home darlin'
And it's nice and dark
And the music's in me
And I'm still real hot

Then you kiss me there
And it feels real good
And I know you'll love me
Like you should!

Oh, you make me feel mighty real
You make me feel mighty real

When the music ended, I usually walked out of the bar alone. The cold sank into my bones like the night fog over the city. A now-familiar feeling of unreality would return, like watching myself in a black and white film, or of rowing against an invisible tide, or of being parched, not in the desert, but at sea.

I wish I could tell you that any single experience revealed the meaning of the meteorite story. That I discovered the hidden truth in some final, queer epiphany. But living, I have learned, involves the constant retelling of our stories, and making new meanings. Sometimes it involves asking questions of our younger selves. If we're lucky, the answers are instructive.

So this is what the meteorite story is about.

It is about a boy in the desert who thought for a long time that something within him lay broken. A boy who couldn't tell his parents his fears, or ask for another try at getting things right. It is also the story of who that boy would become. A man who could hold his parents close as jagged-edged, real people. He would ask them many questions, and get his second chance.

It is the story of a teenager who feared that religion was an instinct that could never be cut out. Who still tried to flog and burn parts of himself anyway. It is about the man who learned that the front of the brain, where the meteorite hit, holds beautiful branches of nerves that allow intelligence and restraint to govern all reflexes. He would choose the best parts of his religion, and see their good uses in the world.

It is the story of a young man who felt always apart. Who danced madly, but feared he'd live anesthetized, waiting for a rare emotion to touch his spirit and body. It is about an adult who discovered, remarkably, others who felt just as numb. He would find non-celestial healers here on earth: musicians and therapists. He would learn that being different could feel less like a liability, and more like a superpower.

It is about my coming to rest in a place that seems the very opposite of the desert.

Just north of the Golden Gate bridge, a small city of houseboats floats in the cool Pacific. The place has its own history of violence between the people on land and those who lived un-moored. These days, cormorants and seals dip peacefully through the waves. Neighbors pass each other on wooden piers between the floating homes. They often wave, eyes wide and smil-ing over masks.

It is 2021, and on most evenings, I sit with my partner on our creaking deck. We like to look up on clear nights. It is the perfect spot, we have discovered, for watching stars and comets go by.

JARID McCARTHY

Exit

The night clear enough to disappear into. The street lights like low-floating drones in summer heat, wavering loose as teeth on a jawbone above us. Somewhere tonight, somebody will huddle close to a humming vent, their body curled toward the exhausting heat, distorted on the face of the road. We'll keep driving, the walls tunneling around us, and the passing light making a dream of everything. My hair will still be wet on the back of my neck. Music on the radio but I won't understand a word, the words suddenly senseless at the momentum of us, the cool silver of your car going East, then South. Directionless in this city and everywhere. What do you want me to say to you? That we'll keep this, the worst of us, that we'll be a pair of lovers slipping through the exit, our shadows going green in the doorway? The desire is not one of absence, of being absent, but of being remembered by people you love. We all want to be seen, even the space we leave behind. When I slip outside to catch my breath, I angle my face to the neon sky and it's just like always, like every time I've had to vanish to breathe, all these moments panicking as a single gasp. I form my escape plan in this gasp, struck by my need to be gone and full of noise at once, this impossible status. I can't keep my plans in order. In the field, your shoes fill with crickets. I watch you turning them over, emptying them, the noisemakers dropping their paper bodies to the cracked earth and curling away into it. They can't move fast enough, escaping something they don't understand. The way you hold the wheel. The way it frustrates against the weight of us. The inside of the car mostly this quiet air afterall.

GIA SHAKUR

RUBBER
Junebug's Dream

There was a bridge I walked across with my slippers. (Unnamed) waited for me with their hands
covered in hunter's gloves. Above us, in soft neon lights read,
"Mule fi free. Rot prevails." I have a notepad in my purse w/ a kill list of my abusers, a handy
book on the striations of bones, a tube of Fenty, a half eaten Heath bar, spilled tobacco, that chain
I snatched from that boy that time who appeared suddenly to dance on the roof of
Sugar Hill's Haberdashery and Dice Hall. I'm learning to fashion my contrition. I knit. I think,
strands of guilt, cords of remorse, my own skin. I knit with needles made from my
grandmother's calf bone. I fasten the hammock over a gaping hole which is actually my
mother's fury formed mouth ..

Then what ?

That man, tall and fine pulled his tongue out and showed me it was nothing but wood and rubber.
Do you know where rubber come from ? Elastic trees in Africa. They scrape the bark with a
machete, rubber water leaks out the side like cum into a beggar's cup, hardens over fire, then the
rubber is laid to refine on bamboo beds … We rubber rot.
I heard about a woman they call god, I hope so. Cause boom , we have long erected stopgap
monuments on the backs of our palms. We, the Grand Marshals of the Forgotten, now standing
on the balcony of a pulpit, as a crew cut manboy named Jesus, hawk in hand, chews the back of
his teeth..

A Dispatch of Care

"Build me a boat" said the girl,
sand rushing from her nose.
Truth will sprout up as angel plants
in cutter lady homes
scraped into our foreheads
with the knuckle bones of the ascended
Bare witness

the god kids will dance
from beer gardens to trap houses
hearts are Velcro
astronaut
will pull off when necessary
(carve the oar for her with your nails)
knots forgotten

** they ate the woman eater dem whole
picked the blood out the lining of their nail beds
with a shaved brow bone
selfless in how they let their flesh
fall into ashy hands
like pulled pork
"how to give yourself to ancestral ligatures
plus other self deprecating rituals"
they lick the back of graceful mouths
laugh until it wraps along the carpet
as a bow **

also :

We found a little god girl on the beach today
It started with Monk (who was pissed)
"I nuh machine cyant feel, dummy cyant see
or dog nuh talk."
Junebug The Twohead

conjures girl god
from salt water and nature
eyes black
her teeth are made of whale waste
her mouth is a perfume jar.

"Bring her to Honey Bun ave -"
said Seed the Hothead.
"Where the 'ooman food,
men crab dangling from their jaw."

Choir

You have a way of pulling the wings
out of my back with your teeth
nah fuck that
You dont get no verses
My ribcage a glasshouse
Choir of flower skulls fly out
You dance in with a helmet and your hands are hot

You the road march king this Summer
rolling my legs under my knees
held my neck the tightest as I said my prayers
smiles thin out over
pale Hennessey and
black tea

Sweep me up
hollow air off your tongue
curl my eyes at them tall tells
you think you doing something
when I wash the money off my skin
soak the blue light, lockers and makeup off my backside

I keep you at distance
nose down like yuh airborne
you asked how i looked dead as your soul escaped through my lips
but im a lover
and love not doing me nothing
so i do my 'love' shit in the corner like an animal
scratching
scraping my feet on the ground
shaking the dirt off my knuckles

ahn you
want a medal
fi cutting yuh hands on stained glass
and tonguing the wound
yuh look for that.

XANDRIA PHILLIPS

It's Not Like the Movies

You begin to see exact forms matriculate, hosed down
like cars in a lot. This is where your people exist
without function or care. I don't need to hear Thom Yorke's voice
to call this dirge existential, though your crisis is more compelling.
Bodies like yours can neither stop dying nor succumb to death
entirely. What is refusal to programmed consent? I wonder
as your eyes move to the figure of a man suspended taut
and white as a sheet. Blood loops through a tube and into him,
thawing the man with life as a technician initiates heartbeat.
The stringed instruments in the foreground swell as though
their fervor is what pulls the blood to his atriums. In this lab
of artificial life a buffalo learns to walk, a horse with a halo
over-head is steadied for labor, two women embrace to fuck,
while their voyeurs inspire a clutch of revulsion in your lip.
You've finally awoken only to find you live on a billboard.
I touch the screen that fractures you from me.
The difference between us? *I was born. You were made.*
Still, somehow I know the feeling. Someone killed you
one thousand times because they were scared of dying once.

Anthony Aguero is a queer writer in Los Angeles, CA. His work has appeared, or will appear, in *Carve Magazine*, *Rhino Poetry*, *14 Poems*, *Redivider Journal*, *Maudlin House*, and others. He has received two Pushcart Prize nominations and has his first forthcoming collection of poetry, *Burnt Spoon Burnt Honey*, with Flower Song Press.

Mary Angelino's poetry is forthcoming in *Arkansas International* and in *New York Quarterly*'s anthology, *Without a Doubt*. Her recent publications include the *Southern Humanities Review*, where she received an honorable mention for the 2019 Auburn Witness Poetry Prize, *Rattle*, *Cincinnati Review*, and the *Best New Poets 2017 & 2015* anthologies. She is an Associate Professor of English at College of the Canyons in Santa Clarita, California.

Honora Ankong is a queer Cameroonian-American poet and writer. Her works exist to complicate and expand narratives of Blackness, immigaration, displacement, queer identity, &. Her words can be found at *Lolwe*, *Mineral Lit*, *Glass*, *The Maine Review*, *storySouth*, and elsewhere. She is a 2020 Pushcart prize nominee and has been featured by Poetry Daily. You can find her on twitter @honooraa and at her website honoraankong.com

Àkpà Árinzèchukwu is an Igbo writer. Their work has appeared in *Kenyon Review*, *Prairie Schooner*, *The Southampton Review*, *Poetry Review*, *Adda*, *Fourteen Poems*, *Arc Poetry*, *Clavmag*, *A&U magazine*, *Middle House Review*, *Lumiere Review*, *Transition*, *Pulp Literature* and elsewhere. They were a finalist for Black Warriors Review Fiction Contest 2020.

Nefertiti Asanti is a poet born and raised in the Bronx and a recipient of fellowships and residencies from the Watering Hole, EmergeNYC, Lambda Literary, Anaphora Arts, Winter Tangerine, and the Hurston/Wright Foundation. Nefertiti is also a 2021 PEN America Emerging Voices fellow. Currently, Nefertiti serves as prose poetry editor of *Stellium Literary Magazine*.

Gwen Aube is a trans girl poet and vandal from Windsor, Ontario. Her work has appeared in *HAD*, *Lammergeier Magazine*, and *Zed Press*. She can be found on instagram as @gwendolyssa.

Lemia Monét Bodden hails from the San Francisco Bay Area. She received her BFA from New York University in Film Production. A photographer since she was 12 years old, Lemia has had her work in over 50 exhibitions, including The United Nations, Momenta Art, New York Photo Festival, DUMBO Arts Festival, MPLS Photo Center, Freies Museum Berlin, Vox Populi, Root Division, ACUD MACHT NEU Galerie, ARLES 2018, Altonaer Museum Hamburg, and Ferencvarosi Gallery in Budapest, Hungary.

Cherri is a 2020 Lambda Literary Fellow and has been published in Catamaran Literary Reader and Shirley Magazine. She earned her MFA from Florida Atlantic University, where she completed her first collection of stories. A native of the Midwest, she is now a Floridian who lives between an ocean and a swamp. https://www.cherribuijk.com/

[sarah] Cavar is a PhD student, writer, and critically Mad transgender-about-town, and serves as Managing Editor at Stone of Madness Press and founding editor of swallow:tale press. Author of three chapbooks, *A HOLE WALKED IN* (Sword & Kettle Press), *THE DREAM JOURNALS* (giallo lit), and *OUT OF MIND & INTO BODY* (Ethel Press, forthcoming 2022), they have also had work in *Bitch Magazine, Electric Literature, The Offing, Santa Fe Writer's Workshop*, and elsewhere. Cavar lives online at www.cavar.club and tweets @cavarsarah.

Em Dial is a queer, triracial, chronically ill poet and educator born and raised in the Bay Area of California. A 2022 Kundiman Fellow and recipient of the 2020 RBC/PEN Canada New Voices Award and the 2019 Mary C. Mohr Poetry Award, her work appears in *Sonora Review, Tinderbox Poetry Journal, Crab Fat Magazine*, and elsewhere.

Tarik Dobbs is an Arab American queer writer & artist born in Dearborn, Michigan. Their visual poems appear in *American Poetry Review, Best of the Net*, & *Poetry Magazine*. Dobbs is Assistant Editor of *Great River Review* and helps out at Poetry.onl. Dobbs's poetry chapbook, *Dancing on the Tarmac*, was selected by Gabrielle Calvocoressi (Yemassee, 2021).

Saúl Hernández is a queer writer from San Antonio, TX and was raised by undocumented parents. Saúl has an MFA in Creative Writing from The University of Texas at El Paso. He's a finalist for Palette Poetry 2020 Spotlight Award. His work is forthcoming/featured in *Poet Lore, Cherry Tree, PANK Magazine*, and among others.

Silas Jones is a writer from Arizona and Washington state. Their work has appeared in the *Wilder Voice, Hobart*, and is forthcoming in Icefloe Press' *Pandemic Love Anthology*. They are based in Brooklyn, but try not to write about that.

Kei Kaimana [they/them] is a disabled nonbinarytrans writer, independent scholar, and artist of Native Hawaiian and Black descent. They work across form, building stories for BIPOC futures that center our historic multidimensionality. Kei was born in Texas, and raised across the United States. They live in a sickening body on stolen land, with a genius crew of interrelated species.

Z Kennedy-Lopez is a word-slinger and sometimes-educator who writes a lot about animals, bodies, queerness, and apocalypses. Their work appears in *Autostraddle, Hobart Pulp*, and other publications, and has received support from the Tin House Summer Writers Workshop and Writing by Writers workshop series. Z reads for *Atticus Review* and can be found digitally @ queerbooksloth on Instagram and Twitter.

Kendra Mack (she/her) is a queer millennial writer from New England. She studies Creative Writing & Literature at Harvard Extension School and graduated from the University of New Hampshire. Find her at kendramackwrites.com or tweeting @kendramack.

Jarid McCarthy is a poet and theater artist residing in Southern California. His work has appeared or is forthcoming in *The Baltimore Review, SURFACES.cx, Night Music Journal,* and *Old Youth Magazine.* He is the creator of Empty Room, an experimental online theater project.

A four-time Moth StorySLAM winner with work published in *Slate, Nerve,* and *The Blue Mesa Review,* **Molly McCloy** lives in Tucson with her wife, Rebecca Curtiss and their dog, Princess Pinwheels of the Purple Mountains. She is currently seeking representation for her memoir manuscript *Nine Grudges.* Find out more at mollymccloy.com

Freesia McKee (she/her) writes poetry, prose, and genres in-between about empathy, apathy, power, and movement. She's the essays editor at *South Florida Poetry Journal,* a regular contributor to the Ploughshares Blog, and is working on a book of ecopoetry. Freesia welcomes you to connect with her online at freesiamckee.com or through Twitter at @freesiamckee.

John Moran teaches English at a Miami high school teeming with hipster rabbis, aloof iguanas, and spontaneous student mosh pits. His work has appeared in *Cosmonauts Avenue, Little Star, Southern Cultures, Subtropics,* and elsewhere. He received a PhD in cultural anthropology from Stanford and an MFA in fiction from Brown, and is a proud product of Tallahassee's public schools.

noor is a poet trying to live in the world—currently in West Philly. she thinks the truth exists. she's a fellow of Callaloo and The Watering Hole. her work has been/will soon be published with *Muzzle, DIAGRAM, ANMLY,* and others. her chapbook, *PRAISE TO LESSER GODS OF LOVE,* was published by Glass Poetry Press in 2019

Kyle Okeke is an economics major and creative writing minor at the University of Houston and has appeared or will appear in the literary journals *Glass: a Journal of Poetry, Foglifter,* and *The New Southern Fugitives,* among others. He tweets @kyleohpoetry.

Cantrice Janelle Penn (they/them/she/her) is a queer Black writer, ever-evolving anti-colonial copyeditor, and overall language blerd whose work has been published in various publications, including *Kweli, Apogee, As/Us,* and *Cunjuh.* Their writing can be found at cantricejanellepenn.com.

Xandria Phillips is a poet and visual artist from rural Ohio. The recipient of a Whiting award, and a LAMBDA Literary Award for their book *HULL* (Nightboat Books 2019), they have received fellowships from Brown University, The Wisconsin Institute for Creative Writing and The Center for African American Poetry and Poetics. website: xandriaphillips.com

Dani Putney is a queer, non-binary, mixed-race Filipinx, & neurodivergent writer originally from Sacramento, California. *Salamat sa Intersectionality* (Okay Donkey Press, May 2021) is their debut poetry collection. Dani's poems appear in outlets such as *Cosmonauts Avenue, Grist & Pedestal Magazine*, among others. Their body is made of Nevada sand. Twitter: @daniputney Website: www.daniputney.com

jamal rashad (he/they) is a poet, editor, and succulent enthusiast. They are primarily interested in using blues and language as an entry point to larger discussions around queerness and embodiment. jamal is a Watering Hole Fellow and has served as an editor for *African Voices Magazine* and the anthology of queer poetry: *Imagoes*. jamal's work has been/will be published in *Big Wash, Foglifter Journal, Ina: A QTBIPOC Queer Erotic Anthology, Queerbook*, and *Ramblr Magazine*. jamal holds a BA in Africana Studies from San Francisco State University and lives in Washington DC. IG: @artinthecourtoftheblackfag. Twitter: @jamalrashadpoet

sage received their MFA in Creative Writing from Saint Mary's College of California. Their poems appear in *North American Review, The Rumpus, Pittsburgh Poetry Review, Penn Review, Drunk Monkeys*, and elsewhere. They live in Kansas. They can be found on Twitter @sagescrittore.

Zak Salih lives in Washington, DC. His writing has appeared in *Crazyhorse, The Rumpus, The Millions, The Chattahoochee Review, The Florida Review, the Los Angeles Review of Books*, and other publications. His debut novel, *Let's Get Back to the Party*, released in February 2021 by Algonquin Books. Twitter: @ZMSalih1982; Instagram: @zakigrams; Website: zaksalih.com

Jasmine Sawers is a Kundiman fellow and graduate of Indiana University's MFA program whose work appears in such journals as *Ploughshares, AAWW's The Margins, SmokeLong Quarterly*, and more. Sawers serves as Associate Fiction Editor for *Fairy Tale Review* and debuts a collection of flash through Rose Metal Press in 2022. Originally from Buffalo, Sawers now lives and pets dogs outside St. Louis. Learn more at jasminesawers.com and Twitter @sawers.

Gia Shakur is a writer and visual artist based in Harlem, NY. Her poetry has been featured in *Guttermag, Foglifter 5.1, Rigorous Magazine, Sinister Wisdom, Joint Literary Magazine, Broadkill Review* and *Grungecake*. Her work centers Black women and girlhood. It focuses and is a response to colorism, class, mental health, and misogynoir. She is currently enrolled in the SUNY Purchase Creative Writing Program. She is an inaugural graduate fellow of The Watering Hole and an alumnus of Winter Tangerine and The Hurston Wright Foundation.

RaJon Staunton is a queer Black writer from West Virginia. Their writing appears or is forthcoming in *Hobart, The Lumiere Review, Foglifter Journal,* and *100 Days in Appalachia,* among other places. RaJon currently serves as a Curatorial Editor for Poets Reading the News and is a finishing their degree in Creative Writing at Marshall University in Huntington, WV.

Mar Stratford is a fourth year student in the University of Arkansas Creative Writing MFA program and friend to all animals. Find zir online at mar-stratford.com or twitter.com/mar_stratford.

Nico Tangorra is a 5'7" Cancer Sun with a bad attitude and a Master's degree. He lives in Chicago. Twitter: @NicosTwtAccount Instagram: @tico.nangorra

Gwendolyn Wallace was born and raised in Danbury, Connecticut, and recently graduated with a degree in the history of science and medicine from Yale University. Along with her creative nonfiction, she is also the author of two forthcoming picture books. Her art practices and research are based in Black feminisms, health justice, and ecomemory work. Gwendolyn was the winner of the 2021 Elizabeth Alexander Creative Writing Award. She can usually be found gardening, exploring used bookstores, or listening to the radical impulses of young children.

Candace Williams is a black queer nerd living a double life. By day, they're a seventh-grade language arts educator. By night, they're a poet. *The Dark Diary,* their first full-length poetry manuscript, was a 2018 National Poetry Series finalist and is forthcoming from GRIEVE-LAND. Their chapbook, *Spells for Black Wizards,* was a 2017 TAR Chapbook Series winner and published by the Atlas Review.

Spencer Williams is from Chula Vista, California. She is the author of the chapbook *Alien Pink* (The Atlas Review, 2017) and has work featured in *Muzzle, Apogee, PANK,* and *Bright Wall / Dark Room.* She received her MFA in creative writing from Rutgers University-Newark. She is currently a PhD student in Poetics at SUNY, Buffalo.

Bessie Flores Zaldívar is a queer writer from Tegucigalpa, Honduras. She's a Tin House 2021 alumni and her work can be found in *CRAFT, PANK, F(r)iction, Palette Poetry,* and elsewhere. Bessie's fiction has been selected for Best of the Net 2020. Her chapbook, *Rain Revolutions,* is forthcoming with Long Day Press. Website: bessiefzaldivar.org Twitter: bessieflores Instagram: bfzaldivar

Tauheed Zaman (he/him) is an immigrant, physician, and queer writer. He grew up in Bangladesh, Nigeria, and various parts of the Middle East. He lives on a houseboat in the Bay Area and sings with the San Francisco Gay Men's Chorus. IG: @agentmowgli

www.ingramcontent.com/pod-product-compliance
Lightning Source LLC
Chambersburg PA
CBHW080913190726
48294CB00009B/2073